More All-of-a-Kind Family

More All-of-a-Kind Family

by Sydney Taylor

ILLUSTRATED BY MARY STEVENS

A YEARLING BOOK

Published by
DELL PUBLISHING CO., INC.
1 Dag Hammarskjold Plaza
New York, N.Y. 10017
Copyright © 1954 by Sydney Taylor
All rights reserved.
ISBN: 0-440-45813-7
Published by arrangement with Follett Publishing Company

Printed in U.S.A.
Eighth Dell Printing—July 1980

MPC

To my other mother and father,
Fanny and Simon Taylor

Lena the Greena

"Wow!" GERTIE EXCLAIMED, "look at the long line of horses and carriages!"

"You have to have a lot of carriages for a wedding," said middle sister Sarah.

"But so many! They must be awful rich!"

"Nah! Everyone spends a lot of money on a wedding," observed Henny.

"C'mon! We don't want to miss the bride!" Charlotte yelled, catching hold of Gertie's arm.

Sarah skipped along at their heels, her loop-tied pigtails bobbing up and down excitedly.

Charlie lay sprawled on the sidewalk, playing with the small wagon Papa had made for him. He had turned it upside down, and his chubby little hands kept spinning the wheels round and round. Suddenly Henny bent down and scooped him up. "Charlie's going to see the lovely bride," she told him.

Charlie let out a vigorous howl. He beat at Henny's chest and struggled to slide out of her arms. "Wanna go down! Down! Want my wagon!"

"We can't take the wagon in all that mob. Leave it here. You'll play with it when we get back." And Henny carried her squirming little brother across the street.

A sizable crowd was gathered around the entrance to the hall. From everywhere children came running, eager to see and admire. The ushers braced themselves and held out their arms to form an open lane for the wedding guests. "Stand back!" they shouted. But the youngsters edged closer and closer, and the lane kept growing narrower.

Already the carriages were discharging the guests. Slowly they paraded up the aisles, up the stairs, to disappear somewhere inside the magic hall. No one bothered much to notice the men, elegant though they were in their full dress. But the ladies! How beautiful they looked in their filmy, floating gowns! The bridesmaids were all dressed alike in pink tulle, with twinkly sequined bodices. Large picture hats framed their smiling faces, and each one carried a small bouquet of matching roses.

"When I get married, I'm going to have a whole bunch of bridesmaids," Charlotte declared.

"Such dresses!" Sarah sighed. "Aren't they lucky?"

Gertie turned to Charlotte. "Aren't you glad it's summer time? If it was winter, we couldn't see their dresses. I'm never going to be married in the winter," she added.

"Me neither," agreed Charlotte. "I'm going to be a June bride."

"I wish we had a wedding to go to," Sarah said wistfully. "In a big hall like this, with lots of people and music and dancing and everything."

"The bride!" "The bride's coming!" The crowd surged forward expectantly. The smaller children jumped up and down and craned their necks for a better view.

Charlie was growing too heavy for Henny. She set him down. But Charlie didn't like it down there. He could hardly breathe. And there was so much noise that it hurt his ears. He wasn't going to stay there any more. He scrambled his way through the sea of legs till at last he stood free at the edge of the curb.

Across the street, he could see his little wagon. It was lonely; it was waiting for Charlie to come back and play with it. He stepped into the gutter.

Down the street a horse and wagon clattered into sight. Charlie neither saw nor heard. His little legs kept toddling steadily onward.

A sudden piercing shriek tore the air! Heads turned in swift alarm. "What's the matter?" "What happened?"

The voice screamed again. "The baby! The baby!"

Henny was filled with a sense of dread. Where was Charlie? Just a moment before, he had been hanging onto her dress.

There he was! Alone — in the middle of the street! Henny's breath came in fearful gasps. "Charlie! Come back! Come back, Charlie!" she moaned. She had to get to him. She had to. "Let me through!" she pleaded, sobbingly. "Oh, please, please! It's my brother! I got to get my baby brother!"

But no one seemed to hear. "Charlie!" she screamed. "Go back! Back! Charlie!"

Charlie heard his name being called. He stopped, bewildered. He looked up. Bearing down upon him was a monstrous horse, blowing and puffing and wild-eyed. Its legs were churning up and down in a terrifying blur. The little boy was too frightened even to move.

"Whoa! Whoa!" the driver roared frantically, pulling on the reins with all his might. The wagon teetered crazily. The wheels skidded, sending off sparks as they ground into the cobblestones.

At that instant, a woman dashed into the street. Her arms reached out, clutching at the boy. Together they rolled over and over in a whirl of dust. For a moment, no one could see clearly what was happening.

Then the woman sat up, breathing hard. Charlie, now crying loudly, was clasped protectingly in her arms. People rushed forward.

Murmurs of wonder at her daring beat down around her. "A miracle!" "You're a brave woman!" "So quick you were!" Hands reached down to take the child from her. A man helped

her to her feet. It was the driver. He was deathly pale, but the sweat was pouring from his face. He kept muttering, "Thank God! Thank God!"

Someone asked, "Are you hurt, lady?"

"No. I'm all right," she replied. She slapped at the dust on her skirt and tried to rearrange her disheveled hair. "How's the little boy?" she asked.

"He's fine, "Henny cried out. "You saved him. You're just the bravest person in the whole world!" She began to sob bitterly. "It's all my fault — I didn't watch him. If it hadn't been for you — Charlie might have been killed!"

Scared and shaken as they were, Gertie and Charlotte nevertheless tried to comfort their older sister. "Don't cry, Henny. Charlie's safe."

"See, Henny! I've got him!" Sarah shouted, holding up Charlie, still sobbing. "See! He's fine!"

In a fresh burst of tears, Henny was about to put her arm around Charlie's rescuer, when she noticed a long scratch on the woman's arm. "Oh, look, you're bleeding!" she exclaimed. "You must come upstairs and let us take care of it. And Mama can fix this big rip in your blouse too. Anyway, she'll want to meet you and thank you for what you did."

The woman hesitated. "It's nice you're asking me."

"Please!" Gertie added her plea. "We like it when there's company in our house."

The woman smiled, and the corners of her full mouth turned up charmingly, her cheeks rounding out like two rosy apples. "All right, I come," she said. She pulled the torn and soiled blouse down over her full bosom and tucked it more firmly into the belt of her broadcloth skirt.

"She's fat," Gertie whispered, as they followed behind.

"Sh-sh-h!" admonished Charlotte. "She's not fat! She's just sort of roly-poly. And anyway, she's a wonderful lady!"

Mama shook her head despairingly over her younger brother. "Hyman," she said reprovingly, "you come to pay us a visit and see how you look! No shave. Your suit looks like you slept in it — a button hanging by a thread. At least you could put on a clean shirt! And your shoes, when did they last see a shine? *Schlumper* (untidy one)!"

Uncle Hyman grinned uncomfortably. "Here," he said, handing Mama a paper bag. "A whole dozen eggs. Fresh from the country." He walked over to his favorite spot in front of the kitchen stove. Hands clasped behind his back, toes turned out, he swayed his short chunky body from side to side, his small blue eyes twinkling good-naturedly.

Such a good soul, thought Ella. He never comes empty-handed.

Mama set a platter of fat slices of salty herring on the big round kitchen table. Uncle Hyman sniffed appreciatively. "Mmm! What could be better than a tasty piece of schmaltz herring? Just to smell it gives one an appetite. There's maybe a boiled potato to go with it?"

Mama smiled. "Yes. Boiled potatoes and sour cream."

"Good, good!" Uncle Hyman rubbed his hands together. His ruddy face glowed.

Ella laughed. "Oh, Uncle Hyman! Here, give me your coat, and I'll sew on the button."

"See what a good niece I have!" Uncle Hyman addressed himself to the stove.

"It would be better if you had a good wife to sew your buttons on," Mama remarked dryly. "Old bachelor! What are you waiting for?"

"For such a girl that she hasn't been born yet," Uncle Hyman guffawed, still addressing the stove.

Annoyed as she was, Mama couldn't help laughing. "Oh, go and wash up," she ordered, handing him a towel.

Uncle Hyman went over to the sink unwillingly, like a small boy. Slowly he rolled up his shirt sleeves. Soon he was sending streams of water and suds splashing over his head and face, grunting and spluttering loudly all the while.

The children ran up the stairs with a clatter and banging that sent Mama flying to the kitchen door. "Goodness!" she scolded. "You'd think an army was coming!" She stopped, her eyebrows raised inquiringly, as she caught sight of the stranger.

There was a babble of agitated talk. It was hard for Mama to understand what they were trying to tell her — something about Charlie. But gradually the story became clear. Mama's face grew white. She caught little Charlie in her arms and held him tight. Over the top of his curly blond head, her eyes sought the woman's. "How can I ever thank you?" she said.

"There's nothing to thank." The woman smiled at Mama.

Charlie slid out of Mama's arms and caught up his stick horse from the corner. "Giddyap!" he shouted, and rode off.

Henny spoke up. "Mama, the lady's got a big scratch on her arm. And her blouse is all torn, too. She didn't want to come, but we made her. We said you'd fix it up."

"Oh, I'm so happy you came," Mama said warmly. "We'd better wash your arm right away. And we'll put some peroxide on it. Hyman, get away from the sink already!"

"You shouldn't bother," the woman protested. "It's really nothing. Just to wash myself — that's all I would like."

Uncle Hyman took a peek at the woman out of the corner of his eye. Then quickly he pulled the towel over his head and yielded his place at .the sink.

"It's supper time," Mama went on. "I know you must be hungry. You're coming home from work, aren't you? At least let me show my appreciation. Please stay and have supper with us. Unless, of course, you're expected somewhere."

"No," the woman replied, "no one expects me."

"Then it's settled. You'll eat with us. Look, I don't even know your name."

"It's Lena — Lena Cohen."

Mama made the introductions all around.

By the time Papa came home, Lena looked quite present-able, with her blouse neatly mended and her wavy brown hair combed. Of course the story was retold in great detail, and Papa heaped praises on her head.

Supper was very cozy, with friendly conversation shared by everyone. Everyone, that is, excepting Uncle Hyman. Throughout the meal he sat in bashful silence.

"How long are you in America?" Papa inquired of Lena.

"Well, now it's August, 1915. So I'm here already almost two years. But still a greenhorn!"

"Lena the Greena!" Henny sang out.

Mama was aghast, but Lena only laughed. "That's right. Lena the Greena. That's what the girls in the factory call me." Her face sobered. "But I'm lucky. I left before the war started. Who knows what's happening with my people over there. It takes a long time for a letter to come."

"The war is a terrible thing. Please God, we should only be able to keep out of it," Mama said fervently.

"Such a nice, big family," Lena commented. "I see you have only one son."

Papa grinned. "That's right. Five daughters to marry off!"

"Well, you certainly don't have to worry," Lena assured him. "Such good-looking American girls. They'll be grabbed up like hot rolls from a bakery."

After supper, everyone went into the front room. Lena admired the red and green carpet, the lace curtains, the piano polished to a high satiny finish. She remarked, "A room is like a human being. You gotta fix it up it should look nice."

Mama whispered into Uncle Hyman's ear. "You hear, *schlumper?* A nice impression you must be making!"

The evening passed pleasantly. Ella sang. Then Henny, Sarah, and Charlotte took turns entertaining with a little piano piece. Lena applauded each performer heartily. When it was time for her to leave, she kept saying over and over again what a good time she had had.

"In that case," Mama told her, "you must come again. You live far from here?"

"No. I board with an old couple on Pitt Street."

"Well, anyway, it's late. Hyman, you better take Lena home," she directed.

"Who — me?" Uncle Hyman jumped up, startled.

"Oh, that's all right," Lena interrupted quickly. "I can go by myself."

"Oh, no, no! I wouldn't think of it," Uncle Hyman declared loudly.

Everyone stared at him in astonishment. It was the first whole sentence he had uttered all evening.

Secret in the Bookstack

"Oh, stop fussing, Ella," cried Henny impatiently. "We're only going to the library."

Ella adjusted her tam to an even more rakish angle on her shiny black hair and studied herself in the mirror.

"Say, isn't that my tam?" Henny was indignant. "Why aren't you wearing your own?"

"Because yours matches my new skirt. Please let me wear it, Henny."

"Oh, all right. But you might have asked me first. And hurry up!"

Ella flashed her a grateful look. "Thanks. You can wear my black velvet one whenever you want to." She turned back to the mirror for a final glance. "All right. I'm ready."

"It's about time!" Henny grumbled.

Sarah hugged her library book. "Don't you just love Friday afternoons?"

"Uh huh," agreed Gertie.

"Especially all of us going together," added Charlotte.

Lately, however, of all the sisters, no one awaited Friday afternoons more eagerly than Ella. Besides the precious books, the library now held an added interest. She wondered, would he be there today, sitting in his usual place? Chestnut brown hair, waving back from his forehead, the largest, bluest eyes she had ever seen, fringed by long, dark lashes. Wasted on a boy, she decided, but still awfully attractive. He always pretended to be interested in some book, but she knew all the time he was really watching her. For weeks, now, it had been going on.

Inside the library, the girls separated. Ella remained downstairs where the grown-up books were while her sisters raced upstairs to the children's room.

Ella slid her books along the "in desk." Casually she looked about the spacious room. He was there! He knew she had come in, too. She could tell by the way he carefully shifted in his seat. Her black eyes began to dance. Quickly she turned her head away.

"Good afternoon, Miss Martin," she greeted the librarian.

"Hello, Miss Ella. How pretty you look today!"

Ella felt a warm glow of pleasure. "Thank you." She's so nice, Ella thought. She must have been awfully pretty herself when she was young, with such a creamy skin and such beautiful eyes.

Miss Martin handed back the card. "I hope you find something interesting." Her eyes followed the girl into the circulating room, and she saw the young man reading at a table. She smiled to herself.

Lured by an interesting book she had selected, Ella sat down on a stool and soon was lost in its pages. The young man rose from his chair and sauntered over to the section just behind the one where Ella sat reading. From time to time he would poke his head around the corner and stare at her.

Henny came down to pay Ella a visit. "I can't find a single thing upstairs. Just a lot of baby books. Wish I could belong down here. Why do they make you wait till you graduate? Oh, look!" she cried in delight. *"Anne of Avonlea!* That's the sequel to *Anne of Green Gables*. I must read it! Take this one out, Ella."

"I've read it already. Besides, I've picked my two books."

"Please! Didn't I lend you my tam?"

"Yes, but I promised I'd lend you mine in return."

"I don't want your old tam. I want this book!"

Ella sighed. "All right, I'll take it. But I just hate to have to give up either one. Somebody else is sure to take it out.

21

Henny's eyes gleamed. "I tell you what — let's hide it," she whispered. "Some place where no one will find it. I know — with the foreign books! People who read foreign books don't even know English, so they won't bother with it. It'll still be there when we come back next Friday. See?"

The young man had returned to his seat when Henny appeared, but he hadn't turned any pages in his book. Now he raised his head and watched carefully as Henny slipped the precious book into the chosen hiding place.

A moment later he was standing in front of the librarian's desk. "Could I please have a piece of paper?" he inquired. His face reddened slightly. "Uh — I want to write something."

Miss Martin tore a sheet off a pad. "Will this do?"

"Yes, ma'am. Thanks." He went back to his seat.

Alas, what Henny and Ella did not know was that library shelves are checked continually. The following morning, first thing, Miss Martin went through the stacks, patiently rearranging the books and putting them back where they belonged. Now how did this book get on the German shelf, she wondered? She pulled it out. A neatly folded piece of paper protruded from its pages. Oh, dear, she thought, people are always leaving things in books. She smoothed it out and began to read.

Dear Ella,

I suppose you're surprised that I know your name. I heard your sisters calling you. I think it's a very pretty name.

I realize I'm being very forward writing you like this since we haven't been formally introduced. Please don't be angry. Seeing you in the library all these past weeks, I feel I already know you.

I want so much to talk to you. Somehow, I know we have a lot in common. One thing we're already certain of — we both like to read. Please, Ella, I should like to be your friend.

Some of my friends are going roller skating in the park this Sunday afternoon. Would you like to come along?

Hopefully,

Jules Roth.

Hmm. So that's why he wanted the piece of paper, Miss Martin thought. Such a sweet letter. He's a nice boy. Well, it's against the rules, but —. Carefully she put the note back and replaced the book where she had found it. Better a broken rule than a broken heart, she said to herself, with a little laugh.

The following Friday, Henny and Ella went immediately to the foreign section. "It's here!" Henny cried. "What did I tell you? Well, help yourself. I'm going upstairs. Maybe I'll find something good, for a change."

As Ella pulled the book down, the paper fluttered out from between its leaves. Curious, she picked it up and unfolded it. She read it once, twice, three times. Two bright spots of color flamed in her cheeks. Excitement sparkled in her dark eyes. Her very first letter from a boy! She tucked it into the pocket of her middy blouse, away from the inquisitive eyes of her sisters. Her head in the clouds, she went back to the English section.

Across the room, the young man looked up eagerly from his book. Ella smiled ever so slightly; the nod of her head was ever so tiny. The young man stood up and began to walk towards her.

Behind her desk, Miss Martin smiled understandingly.

Yom Kippur, Day of Atonement

IT WAS EARLY in October. In a few days, the solemn festival of Yom Kippur would be observed. Yom Kippur, the day when people try to make up for their sins by fasting and prayer. The day when they ask God to grant them pure hearts so that they may lead better lives in the year to come. The day when they promise to help those less fortunate than themselves.

"This time I'm going to fast a whole day," Sarah declared stoutly.

"It's easy to say that now, when you're not hungry," commented Henny.

"I could never fast a whole day!" Charlotte cried. "I'd just die!"

"You don't have to fast a whole day," Ella assured her. "Papa says till twelve o'clock is plenty for children."

"The only one in the family who doesn't have to fast even a minute is Charlie," remarked Gertie.

"He does, too," Henny said, grinning. "He has to fast between meals, doesn't he?"

"Think of Papa and Mama all day in the synagogue without a drop of food or water!" Ella said. "Which reminds me. If Mama is to have flowers for Yom Kippur this year, we'd better get busy, and order them now. We can't do any buying on the holiday."

"Let's go today." suggested Sarah. "Have we got enough money?"

"Sure! We're rich! With fifty cents from my two piano pupils and with what you all chipped in, we have seventy-five cents. We can get a big bouquet for that. She'll be proud!"

"Flowers on Yom Kippur," mused Charlotte. "Flowers always make you glad when you're sad."

"They'll help Mama fast," said Gertie. "Every time she gets a little hungry, she can smell the flowers."

It was a long walk, but their happy errand made the way seem short. A visit to the flower shop was a rare treat. Once inside the store, the children roamed about in delight, feasting their eyes on the beauty around them. They breathed in deeply the heavenly scents, and tenderly touched the velvety flower petals. With such a variety to choose from, they could not make up their minds. Mr. Pappas, the owner, finally offered to decide

26

for them. "You just leave everything to me. I'll fix you the nicest bouquet you ever saw!"

"With lots of ferns all around?" Charlotte asked.

"Sure, sure. Lotsa ferns!"

So Ella turned over the money, and it was arranged that the bouquet would be delivered on Yom Kippur morning.

"Not before nine thirty," she warned. "We don't want Mama to see the flowers before we bring them to the synagogue.

And not later, either, because we have to go to synagogue ourselves."

Mr. Pappas gave his word, and the children went home.

On the way home, Sarah reminded Henny, "You'll have to make up with your friend Fanny. You know it's a sin to be mad at anybody on Yom Kippur."

"That's fine with me," Henny answered brightly. "Then I'll be able to ask her to lend me her brand-new skates."

That night Uncle Hyman had supper with the family. When he was about to leave, Mama reminded him, "Remember, Hyman, I expect you Yom Kippur eve."

"Don't worry, Mama," Papa said. "A Yom Kippur eve supper he wouldn't dream of missing."

Uncle Hyman grinned. He stood at the door, awkwardly twirling his hat in his small chunky hands as if reluctant to go. "Er — er, maybe —" he began. He stopped, embarrassed, his eyes avoiding Mama's. He swayed back and forth, staring at his shoes. "You think maybe — if — if I brought an extra whole dozen eggs —." Finally he blurted out, "Maybe we could invite a certain party also?"

Mama's eyes twinkled. "Hyman, what certain party would you mean?" she asked innocently.

Uncle Hyman's face turned very red. Mama waved a

hand at him. "Don't bring the eggs, Hyman. Just bring Lena. We'd love to have her."

"Uncle Hyman's got a girl!" Henny cried out, giggling.

Smiling sheepishly, Uncle Hyman came back into the room. Suddenly he thrust a fistful of pennies onto the table. "Here, girls," he called out, "buy yourselves something."

Shouting with glee, the children pounced upon the money. When they turned to thank Uncle Hyman, he was already gone.

Yom Kippur eve, and all over the East Side, factories and stores closed down. The market places grew still, no peddlers cried their wares from pushcarts and stands; no horses and wagons threaded their way through the narrow streets. In their homes, Jews were preparing for this most important holiday. In Mama's house, all was in readiness — the children in their holiday clothes, the table set for a feast, and from the simmering pots on the kitchen stove came appetizing smells.

Mama beamed approvingly at Uncle Hyman. He looked so scrubbed and neat. He was wearing a clean white shirt with bright red garters holding up the sleeves and bright red suspenders to match. "Firemen's suspenders!" he boasted, snapping them proudly. Mama nodded her head smilingly at Lena. What a difference a woman can make, she thought.

"Come," Papa announced, "we'd better begin. We must be finished eating before the sun sets."

Tonight's dinner was like a banquet. Chicken fricassee first. Then came chicken soup in which fluffy *kreplech* (squares of dough filled with meat) floated temptingly. Uncle Hyman and Lena fell to shoveling vigorously with their soup spoons, drinking down the hot savory liquid with gusto.

Roast chicken and carrots followed. And then Mama brought out a steaming noodle pudding, rich and sweet, with lots of almonds and raisins. Fruit compote next, tea, and last of all, sugar-and-cinnamon-topped cookies.

"Oh, I'm so full!" Ella cried, folding her hands over her stomach. "I just can't believe that I'll be hungry tomorrow."

"That's the way it is with people," Lena said. "Either they feast to death or fast to death."

It was time now for Mama to light the holiday candles. Everyone was quiet as she recited the special holiday blessing. They were extra quiet as they watched her touch a match to the wick in a special candle-filled glass — the memorial candle. This light would burn through the night and all through the next day, in memory of loved ones who were dead.

Now Papa blessed his children, one by one. "May God bless you. May he grant you a good life and a good and under-

standing heart, that you choose the righteous way of life with faith and good deeds."

It seemed strange for the children to go to synagogue at night. In the street Gertie linked her arm through Charlotte's as they trotted alongside Lena. "When I was a little girl," Lena said, "my grandpa told me that, on the day of Yom Kippur, the little door of Heaven opens up, and you can see the angels."

"Is that really true?" The two little girls stared up at Lena with wide eyes. "Can you really see them?"

"Tomorrow you'll watch, so you'll see," Lena answered, with an air of mystery.

The synagogue, looking unfamiliar with the lights on, was crowded with devout worshippers. The young children went to sit with Papa and Uncle Hyman. Lena, Ella, and Henny followed Mama behind the curtains to the women's section. The cantor began to sing the old, old prayer, Kol Nidre. Tender and moving, and set to a hauntingly beautiful melody, it touched the hearts of all with great sadness.

That night, when Gertie was brushing her teeth just before going to bed, Charlotte cautioned, "You mustn't swallow the water, Gertie. Not even a single drop. Or it won't count for fasting."

"I'll be careful," Gertie replied earnestly. "I'll spit it right out."

Next morning, a few minutes after Papa and Mama had left for the all-day service, the bouquet of flowers arrived. "Isn't it gorgeous!" Charlotte exclaimed. "Mr. Pappas fixed it up just perfect!" She buried her nose deep in the bouquet. "Mmm-mmm!"

"Let me!" demanded Gertie.

"Close your eyes, Gertie. Then you can smell better," suggested Charlotte.

"Give Charlie a smell," Sarah said. "No, no, Charlie — mustn't touch!"

Finally Ella had to cry a halt. "You'll take all the smell out of them," she complained.

"I want to carry the flowers," Charlotte declared.

"No," Henny told her. "You'll crush them. I'll carry them."

"I won't crush them. I'll be very careful, I promise. Please, Ella, let me carry them just for a little while."

"Then I want a chance too," Gertie insisted.

Everyone wanted to share in the lovely feeling of holding a bouquet of flowers — even Charlie. Ella finally decided that they would take turns while she kept a close watch on the bearer the whole time.

"Mama'll be surprised," said Sarah happily. "We certainly kept the secret. She doesn't suspect she's getting flowers this year."

Up the narrow stairs the children went, tiptoeing into the synagogue. The room hummed with the continual intoning of prayers. It was hot and close, full of the mingled odors of old and yellowing prayer books, prayer shawls, people, and the sharp scent of snuff.

At the entrance to the women's section, Ella bent down and placed the bouquet in Charlie's arms. "Take these to Mama," she whispered. She drew aside the curtain. Little Charlie, his

33

small body almost buried beneath his precious burden, toddled forward slowly, followed by his watchful sisters. Women smiled at the little boy, but he did not notice. His eyes searched only for Mama.

There she was! She was holding out her arms to him, her face alight with joy and pride. Pleased all over himself, Charlie snuggled to her side, offering up the flowers.

"Such a surprise!" Mama murmured. "Dear children, thank you!" She kissed each one of them. Holding the flowers up to her face, she breathed in their sweetness. It made the girls happy for Mama and sorry for all the other mamas who had no flowers to help them through the long, long day.

"Are we in time, Mama?" Ella asked softly.

"Yes. S-s-sh! The memorial services are starting."

Gravely the congregation began to chant the opening words in memory of the dear ones who had died. The children could feel the mournfulness come creeping into their own hearts. All around them, women were sobbing unashamed. And even some of the men wiped their eyes with their handkerchiefs.

On and on the services went, and by noon the younger children were more than ready to break their fast. "I'm so hungry, my stomach is talking," Gertie whispered. And Charlotte rejoined, "Me, I could eat a bear!"

But Sarah remained strong in her resolve to stick it out all day. Mama studied her thin, white face, the faint shadows under her eyes. She stroked Sarah's head. "You fasted long enough my child," she said tenderly. "I'm sure God has already forgiven you your little sins. When you are older, you will fast longer. Papa and I are still here. We'll keep on praying for all of you."

So Sarah went home and ate lunch with the others. And a moment after, it was as though they had never fasted at all.

All through the afternoon, the services continued. When the children returned, the story was being read of how Yom Kippur was celebrated in the Temple in days of old.

Amidst all the splendor in the Temple at Jerusalem, there was one small chamber which boasted no wonderful golden objects, no luxurious hangings. It was considered the Holy of Holies, because it was the place where the spirit of God was thought to rest. The curtains to this room always remained closed. They opened for but one man — the High Priest; for but one day — Yom Kippur.

For a whole week the High Priest prepared himself for this awesome day. He studied with the wise men and other priests. He prayed; he cleansed his body. The last night he did not sleep. With the coming of the dawn, he did not break his fast, but performed the necessary rituals. In the course of the day, he bathed five times and washed his hands and feet ten times.

Then came the moment. He donned a simple white linen gown. He chanted a prayer confessing his sins and the sins of all, and, holding a vessel of burning incense in his hands, he entered the Holy of Holies. The curtains closed behind him.

No one knew what went on in the small chamber, but in the Temple courtyards the priests and, behind them, the congregation of men and women, anxiously watched the circles of smoke rise through the folds of the curtain — watched and prayed.

When the High Priest emerged at last, shouts of joy burst from the lips of the people.

Services were drawing to a close. N'ilah N'ilah — the closing prayer symbolizing the locking of the Temple gates — was being recited. The congregation rose to its feet.

"The Lord He is God!" The Shofar (ram's horn) was sounded once, triumphantly. "Yom Kippur is over!" All were ready now to face the coming year with renewed hope and spirit.

Amid the general rejoicing and well wishing, a young man pushed his way through to where Ella stood with her family.

"Hello, Ella," he said. "How was your fast?"

"It wasn't too bad," Ella replied, flushing. She started talking very fast, giggling a bit. The sisters stared at her. What had gotten into their big sister to make her act so silly all of a sudden? And who was this young man, anyway?

"Who are you?" Henny burst in impudently.

"Henny!" Mama chided, but she did not seem very seriously annoyed. "How about introducing your acquaintance, Ella," she said.

"Oh, excuse me," Ella cried, all flustered. "This is Jules — Jules Roth. Jules, this is my family."

The young man shook hands all around, getting the names mixed up. "It looks like my folks went on ahead without me. Well — er — nice to have met you all. See you later, Ella." He beat a hasty retreat.

"Seems like a nice boy," commented Mama.

"Oh, he's all right," Ella replied in an off-hand manner. Quickly she added with greater enthusiasm. "He's a senior in high school! Jules! Isn't that a beautiful name?"

"Jules!" scoffed Henny. "I bet it's Julius."

"What if it is!" Ella retorted hotly. "I think Jules is much more beautiful. And besides, I like it."

All day long, Gertie and Charlotte had craned their necks in vain searching the sky for the little door to Heaven. Now, as they were walking home with the family, Charlotte pointed upward excitedly. "Look, Gertie! That bright streak of cloud! That's it! It's shaped just like a door!"

Hand in hand, they raced forward, trying to catch a peek underneath. But alas, as they reached the corner of the street, the light faded away.

When the family caught up with them, Gertie wailed, "It got too dark, Papa. They closed it up! We missed the angels!"

Papa smiled sympathetically. "Well, little one, maybe next year."

A Friend in Need

"But why do i have to go to bed so early?" Henny kept insisting.

"Why, why! Always why!" replied Papa. "I've answered that question so many times already. A girl your age needs lots of sleep if she wants to be healthy. If you don't get your rest, you won't do your lessons right. You have trouble enough as it is, keeping up your marks in school."

"But nine thirty is awful early!" Henny protested. "You let Ella stay out till ten thirty."

"For Heaven's sake!" Ella exploded. "Ten thirty is early enough for a girl nearly sixteen years old without your trying to spoil it!"

"Aw, heck!" muttered Henny. "Not a single one of my friends has to be home that early. You treat me like a baby."

"Never you mind about your friends. Their parents will worry about them," Papa answered sharply.

"But it's Saturday night. There's no school tomorrow."

"I know very well what night it is."

"Couldn't you make it ten o'clock, at least?"

Papa shook his head. "No, Henny. I've been very patient with you up till now, no matter how many times you were late before. Now my patience is at an end. I expect you home by nine thirty."

"Nine forty-five, Papa, please!"

"Henny! I said nine thirty, and not one minute more!" Papa was getting angry. He shook his finger at Henny threateningly. "And if you're late this time, you'll get a licking for sure!"

Charlotte couldn't understand why Henny was making such a fuss. "Gertie and I like to go to bed early," she remarked. "We have so much fun."

"Yes," Gertie agreed. "Charlotte makes up such wonderful stories. All about two naughty girls, even better than the Katzenjammer kids; and every night she tells me another chapter. The stories are so exciting that sometimes I just can't wait till it's bedtime!"

Sarah sighed. "Ella and I used to have lots of fun too. Remember, Ella, how we used to fix up our make-believe house? Now most times I have to go to sleep all by myself. When Ella creeps into bed, she puts her cold feet right on top of my warm feet and it wakes me up. But by that time I'm so sleepy I don't feel like talking any more."

Ella put her arm around Sarah's shoulder. "Tell you what," she said consolingly, "my whole crowd's getting together right after supper. I promised I'd be there, but I'll get home real early. Like old times. Okay?"

"Oh yes!" Sarah replied, giving her sister a hug.

"That marcel-waved Jules going to be there tonight?" Henny inquired mischievously.

Ella replied unthinkingly. "No, he won't. He has to stay home and study for exams."

"I thought so!" Henny laughed. "No wonder you're so big-hearted all of a sudden!"

Ella didn't bother to answer.

It was nine-thirty. Charlie lay asleep in his bed, like a small angel. In the girl's room, Gertie and Charlotte had ceased to giggle and whisper in the dark, but Ella and Sarah were still wide awake planning the decoration of a room in blue. In the kitchen Mama and Papa sat reading.

At nine forty-five Papa laid down his newspaper. "The child must be taught a lesson," he fumed. He turned to Mama. "No

41

need for both of us to wait up. Why don't you go to bed? I know you must be tired."

Mama pressed her finger tips against her weary eyes. "I am, a little," she admitted. "But what's the use? I won't be able to sleep till Henny gets home."

"Lie down, anyway," Papa urged. "At least that way you'll get some rest."

"All right, Papa." Mama started for the bedroom. Hand on the doorknob, she hesitated. "You won't be too hard on her? You know how children are. They get to talking, they don't realize the time."

On the kitchen shelf, the clock loudly ticked the minutes away. Ten o'clock! Papa's fingers strummed anxiously on the table. So once again Henny had disobeyed him. Despite everything he had said. Well, tonight she'd get what she deserved! It was long overdue! He stood up, slipped the bolt in the kitchen door shut, turned out the light, and went to bed.

Tonight all of Henny's friends had congregated in Fanny's house. Fanny could play the latest songs on the piano, and the girls gathered around and sang. Most of them could waltz pretty well, too; but they didn't any of them know how to do the new dance called the foxtrot. Fanny's big sister and her boy friend, who were very good dancers, showed it to them. The girls were entranced; everyone wanted to learn. Fanny grew awfully tired thumping out the same tune over and over while each girl had her turn at a dancing lesson.

Afterwards, everyone felt hot and thirsty. "Let's go to Mrs. Blumberg's and buy a penny chocolate soda," suggested Henny. Down in the candy store they stood around sipping the sweet drink slowly, talking and laughing. Before they knew it, Mrs. Blumberg was shooing them out. "Go— go on home already! I gotta close up."

In a flash Henny remembered. She'd given Papa her word! "Is it nine-thirty yet?" she inquired anxiously.

"Nine-thirty it wouldn't be any more tonight," Mrs. Blumberg replied. "It's ten o'clock."

"Ten o'clock!" There were exclamations of dismay. "Oh, am I late!" "I gotta get home!" "So long, everybody!" All the girls made a rush for the door.

Henny caught hold of Fanny's arm as they ran. "Some friend you are!" she said reproachfully. "Why didn't you remind me? I told you I promised my Papa I'd be home by nine-thirty. Boy, will I catch it!"

"What do you think I am, an alarm clock?" Fanny replied.

Henny was worried. "Maybe it won't be so bad. I'm only a half hour late." Papa hardly ever spanked the children. Still, she doubted if she'd be able to escape a licking tonight, especially after she argued about the time. Papa had certainly sounded as if he meant what he said. She searched about desperately for a solution. All at once she had a thought.

"Listen, Fanny, how about coming up to my house?"

"Right now? Are you crazy?"

"Oh, I don't mean to stay. Just come upstairs with me."

"I can't. I have to be home, too. I'm late enough as it is."

"Oh, come on. It'll only be for a few minutes."

44

"What difference would it make if I came along?"

"Well, Papa wouldn't spank me in front of a stranger — I don't think. Then we could sort of explain what happened, and maybe he wouldn't be so angry."

"Well — " Fanny debated with herself for a moment and finally gave in. "All right. But I must go home right away."

The hall lay in utter darkness. The two girls had to grope their way up the stairs. No light streaked through at the sill of the kitchen door, either. "Everybody's asleep already," Henny said in an undertone. Stealthily she turned the knob, her knee pressing against the door. It did not yield. "How do you like that!" she whispered fiercely, "I'm locked out! Now I'll have to bang on the door and wake everybody up."

"Gee, that'll make your Papa madder than ever. I'm going!" Fanny started toward the stairs.

Henny pulled her back. "You can't leave me now," she begged. "You promised! Anyway, I've got an idea."

"What?"

"Ella's and Sarah's bed is right up alongside the wall. I'll knock on the wall for a signal. When Ella hears, she'll understand. She'll open the door for me, and I'll creep into bed without Papa even knowing."

"Do you think she'll hear?"

45

"Sure!" She felt along the wall till she reached the spot where she imagined the bed to be. "Well, here goes," she murmured, tapping out a signal. "Ta ta — ta ta — ta ta ta ta." She paused, then tapped a second time. With her mouth against the wall, she called softly, "Ella! Ella!" The girls held their breath for a moment, waiting.

The door unlatched and opened. A strong arm reached out into the darkness. Without a word, Papa turned his captive over his knee. Whack! Whack! Whack!

"Papa! Please, Papa, stop!" Henny yelled.

Papa went right on with his spanking. Once, twice, three times more. A hand tugged at his sleeve. "Papa! You're hitting the wrong girl. I'm Henny. That's Fanny you've got there!"

Papa's hand stopped in mid-air.

Fanny had been too terrified to utter a sound. Now she started to bawl at the top of her lungs. A light went on in the kitchen, and Mama appeared. "What's going on?" she demanded. She looked down at the bawling Fanny. "And what happened to you?"

Abashed, Papa tried to explain. "It was dark, Mama. I was giving Henny a spanking —"

Mama looked around, puzzled. "Then why is Fanny crying?"

"Well, you see, Mama," Papa stuttered — "I couldn't see it was a mistake — and —"

"He whacked Fanny instead of me," Henny finished for him.

Mama gathered the weeping Fanny into her arms. "Oh, you poor child!"

Papa tried to smile. "You'll have to excuse me, Fanny, dear child. I made a bad mistake. I didn't mean —"

Henny walked over to Fanny and took her hand. She felt awfully guilty, but somehow the whole thing suddenly seemed very funny. She.felt a fit of giggles coming on. She tried to control herself, but it was no use. She just doubled over with laughter. In another moment, Fanny's screwed-up face changed to a smiling one. A moment more, and both Papa and Mama were laughing so hard they couldn't stop.

The sounds of such unusual merriment brought the sisters running, their startled eyes blinking at the light. Mama shooed them in. "Back to your beds! It's late!"

"But why is everyone laughing?" sleepy Gertie asked.

"It's your Papa. Such a way to carry on! He'll have good cause to remember this night. I'll tell you all about it in the morning. Into bed now, every one of you!"

Henny needed no urging. No sense hanging around to remind Papa that he still owed her a licking. "Thanks loads, Fanny," she whispered quickly and skedaddled off to bed.

"Go right home, Fanny," Mama went on. "Your folks must be anxious."

Papa locked the door with what sounded like a sigh of relief.

"Oh, Papa!" Mama shook her head at him in comic distress. "How am I ever going to explain to Fanny's mother?"

48

A Timely Errand

"CAN ANYONE in the class tell time?" asked the teacher. There was no reply. It seemed no one could. Now, that was silly of me, the teacher realized. Of course they can't tell time yet. Some of them are not even eight years old. Just then one small palm waved in the air. "My, Gertie!" the teacher exclaimed in pleased surprise. "You can! How very clever of you!" There was a buzz of admiration from Gertie's classmates.

"Then you can do an errand for me," the teacher went on. "You know the big clock at the other end of the hall? Would you please go and see what time it is and come back and tell us."

Oh, dear! Gertie's conscience shook its finger at her.

Conscience: See, Miss Smarty. That's what happens when you try to show off. Why did you raise your hand? You know very well you can't tell time! Now what are you going to do?

49

Gertie: I don't know. Something made me. Anyway, I
               didn't think she was going to test me out. I just
               thought she was asking. Oh, what shall I do?
Conscience: You could tell her the truth.
Gertie: And have the whole class know! I can't. I just can't.
Conscience: You'll be sorry, you'll see. You'll get pimples all over
               your tongue 'cause you told a lie!

Gertie's heart went thumpety thump. She wanted to put
her head down on her desk for shame. Instead, here were her
feet carrying her down the aisle, across the front of the classroom, and out the door!

She started down the hallway. There it was, a great round
monster high on the wall, its numbers just a jumble of black
on a white face. Slowly she watched the brass pendulum swing
back and forth, back and forth. It was ticking out a mocking
refrain. Tick, tock, tick, tock — You don't know how — to read
a clock! She gulped. Her small face crumpled up, and soon her
tears were making the clock look all blurry.

All at once she noticed a big girl coming towards her.
Maybe she'll be able to help me, Gertie thought hopefully. Hurriedly she wiped her eyes. "Miss," she asked eagerly, "would
you please tell me what time it is?"

"Sure. It's twenty minutes to eleven."

"Oh, thank you!" Gertie cried, her face all sunshiny again. "Twenty minutes to eleven," she repeated. She eyed the clock curiously for a moment, wondering about the mystery of its two hands. Well, she'd better get back to the classroom. Teacher must be wondering what was taking so long. Her feet had wings as she sped down the hall.

Alas, Gertie could not know what trouble she had let herself in for. Every day, thereafter, Teacher would send her out to get the time. And day after day, she would stand beneath the clock, praying that someone — a teacher, a pupil, or perhaps the janitor — would come along. Day after day, the longing to tell the truth and have the whole thing over and done with grew and grew and grew. But it was so hard, so hard! She just couldn't bring herself to do it.

Every afternoon, as soon as she got home from school, she'd rush to the mirror and anxiously examine her tongue. When would the pimples start showing, she wondered fearfully. She was sure she could feel them already, sort of inside the tongue, even if she couldn't actually see them.

Always before, she had told Charlotte everything. Now she was too ashamed. Maybe if Charlotte knew what a big liar she was, she wouldn't even want to be friends with her any more.

Charlotte was so smart. She could tell time. Gertie kept

51

pestering her with questions, but what Charlotte said didn't seem to make any sense. Gertie kept asking and asking, trying desperately to understand. She knew there'd come a day when no one would be in the hall to give her the answer.

She dreaded going to school. She would sit in fear and trembling, waiting for the terrible moment when Teacher would smile at her sweetly and send her out on this most important errand.

Now — today — this very moment, the thing she had feared most was finally happening. She had been under the clock for the longest time. She couldn't stay out much longer. Teacher would surely suspect something. Agonizingly the minutes ticked by. Gertie chewed on her fingernails. She walked up and down, up and down, but there was nobody around — just nobody!

She came back to the clock. If only she had a big rock. She'd smash that old clock's face in a million pieces! Then no one could ever read it again, not even Teacher herself.

"You mean old face," she exclaimed tearfully. "Why don't you talk to me?" Then she noticed the small hand was on the eleven. Something like a spark hopped across her forehead. Little wheels of thought started whirring. Charlotte had said the small hand is for the hours. So it must be eleven o'clock! The big hand wasn't too far away. It was on the 2. Now what had she said about that? Each little dot you counted as one minute, starting from the 12, down the right side. That was it! All aquiver, Gertie began counting. It added up to ten dots. Why — why — then it must be ten minutes after eleven! Her heart gave a leap.

Just a minute, an inner voice cautioned. Not so fast. Don't get so excited. You'd better make sure first. But how?

"Would you like to know the time?" a gentle voice asked.

Gertie jumped, startled. There standing beside her was just the most important person in the whole school — Miss Phillips, the principal! Gertie's voice shook. "Is it — is it — ten minutes after eleven?" she stammered.

"That's right," Miss Phillips answered with a smile. "That's very good for such a little girl."

"Oh, yes, I can tell time! I can really and truly tell time! Miss Phillips, don't you think this is the loveliest clock in the whole world?" Gertie laughed all over herself. Without waiting for a reply, she whizzed down the hall, leaving Miss Phillips staring after her in puzzled amusement.

Festival of Lights

"Latkes for supper!" Henny's mouth watered.

There was an instant chorus of "Yum, yum!"

Mama smiled. "Well, children, it seems everybody loves *latkes*. And Hanukkah's the time to eat them. Who wants to grate the potatoes?"

"Me! Me!" the younger ones cried.

So Mama let Charlotte and Gertie take turns. When they grew tired, Ella and Henny took over. In a little while, the large mixing bowl was full to the brim with mushy potato liquid.

Then Sarah grated the onions. "Ooh, it bites my nose and eyes!" she complained. She grated very fast, her face all screwed up and the tears flowing.

"Look! Sarah's crying. She must be sorry for the onions," Henny said, grinning.

Now into the bowl went eggs, matzo flour, salt and pepper. Mama stirred and stirred the mixture. By this time the oil in the frying pan was bubbling hot. It sizzled a welcome to the spoonfuls of pancake mix Mama fed it. Soon a delicious aroma spread through the room. The children hung over the stove, eager for a taste of the very first hot potato pancake that would come off the fire.

My, it was good! All crispy, crunchy outside, all tasty, chewy on the inside! It disappeared too quickly in the mouth, rushed down to the tummy, leaving them with a craving for more. Mama knew she'd have to keep careful watch, or there'd be none left for supper.

"Here comes Papa, now."

"Just in time, I see," Papa said, as he caught a whiff of the appetizing odor.

Papa was gay, laughing and joking with the children as he washed up. Tonight the whole family was gay. It was the time for gladsomeness. It was the first night of Hanukkah — Festival of Lights — the happy holiday right in the midst of December's bleakness. Jews everywhere celebrate Hanukkah with song, games, and parties, and the giving of gifts and money.

Ella had polished the brass Menorah till it shone like a mirror. It had been placed on the top shelf of the whatnot, its eight little holders all in a row ready to receive the slim, golden yellow candles Papa had bought especially. In the middle, set up high above the others, was the *shamosh* (sexton) candle. Its flame would be used to kindle all the others.

The children grouped themselves around Papa as Mama lifted Charlie onto a chair. Papa placed a candle in the first holder of the Menorah. Then, holding the lighted *shamosh,* he turned to Charlie. "Would you like to light it?" he asked.

Charlie jumped up and down. "Yes, yes! Charlie wanna light the candle!" he cried, his little hands reaching out eagerly.

Papa's firm hand guided his son's towards the wick of candle number one. Bright and shining, it sprang to light, matching the glow on Charlie's face.

Papa's voice was deep and reverent. "Praised be Thou, O Lord our God, Ruler of the Universe, who has commanded us to kindle the Lights of Hanukkah."

Over two thousand years ago, Antiochus, King of Syria, sent forth a mighty army into Palestine, to force the Jews to give up their religion. It was forbidden to hold services in the Temple of Jerusalem, and God's house itself was turned into a Greek Temple. The Jews who refused to submit were destroyed. They were the first religious martyrs known to history.

There rose up a strong and courageous man; Judas Maccabeus was his name. He roused his people to fight for freedom. For three long years, the struggle raged, until at last victory was theirs. In triumph, the brave Jewish soldiers returned to the city of Jerusalem.

When the pagans had occupied the Temple, they had defiled it by the sacrifice of unclean animals. Anxiously, the priests searched for some unpolluted oil to rekindle the Menorah (perpetual light). All they could find was one tiny vessel of oil, its seal still unbroken. This would be enough to last only one day.

But, by a miracle, the scant supply lasted eight full days — long enough for olives to be gathered and pressed and fresh oil made!

Once again holy services could be held in the Temple, with

songs and prayers offered up to God. Candles gleamed in the homes, and even the streets of the city were lit. For eight days the celebration continued. Ever since, each year, the candle lighting ceremony is repeated for eight nights, with a candle added each night.

"Tomorrow I want to hold the *shamosh* and light the two candles," Gertie said.

"Six children and Papa and Mama makes eight." Sarah had it all figured out. "It'll come out exactly right."

"Yes," Papa nodded. "Everybody will have a chance. Ella, sing for us."

So Ella sang "Rock of Ages," and in a little while, the whole family joined in.

> Rock of Ages, let our song
> Praise thy saving power;
> Thou amidst the raging foes
> Wast our sheltering tower.

Mama beamed at Papa. "Now, Papa?"

The children smiled at each other. They knew what was coming. Papa pulled out his change purse. "I'm afraid there isn't much Hanukkah money inside," he declared in mournful tones, but the girls could see that his eyes were shiny with teasing. Now he was distributing pennies, two of them to each child!

"So much money!" breathed Charlotte.

"Wait till we visit the relatives!" Henny added. "Then we'll really be rich!"

Ella was provoked. "Henny, you're not going to go around collecting! That's all right for the kids."

"Is that so?" Henny tossed her head. "Well, I'm never going to be too old to collect presents — especially money!"

Mama put a hasty end to the argument. "Come now, children," she called out, "or the *latkes* will get cold!"

On Sunday afternoon the family was about to leave for a Hanukkah party at Aunt Rivka's house. "Bundle up tight," advised Papa; "it's cold outside."

"It feels like more snow," Mama added. "We'd better take our rubbers. Ella, you get the umbrellas."

"Do we have to drag umbrellas?" Henny questioned. "It's so much fun to walk in the snow."

"Well, all right then, just rubbers for everyone," Mama decided. "And one umbrella for me. I don't want to spoil my good hat."

With Papa and Charlie in the lead, the family was soon on its way. The younger girls had a hilarious time jumping up and down the hills of snow piled up against the curb. "Take care! You'll dirty your dresses!" Mama warned.

"Mama," asked Henny, "is Uncle Hyman bringing Lena to the party?"

"I think so. Why?"

" 'Cause if he does, it means we'll get an extra present," said Henny gleefully. "Now that Uncle Hyman goes around with her, we don't see him so often. I miss him."

"Him or his pennies?" Ella asked.

Henny grinned. "Both."

"Lena isn't a relative. She doesn't have to give us anything," Sarah reminded her sister.

"Mama, do you see the way Lena eats?" Gertie asked. "She cuts her meat with the knife in her left hand and the fork in her right. Just the opposite!"

"That's the European way," Mama explained. "Very sensible, too. They don't have to keep switching their forks all the time."

"But Lena eats with her knife, too. She uses it like a shovel. Do they do that in Europe too?" Charlotte asked.

"And the way she hangs over her plate," Henny went on. "Like somebody was going to take it away from her."

"She's probably still not used to having plenty of good food," Mama said. "Things weren't so easy for Lena in the old country."

"Well, that's one thing she and Uncle Hyman have in common," Ella observed. "They sure love to eat."

"And her English is so funny, too," Charlotte added.

"That's because the language is still strange to her," Mama said, less patiently. "Do you know she can speak several languages? Russian, Polish, Jewish. Any of you speak Polish as poorly as you seem to think Lena speaks English?"

Mama's words made the girls feel a little foolish. They fell silent. But then Henny started chuckling. "When she walks, I always feel like saying, "Here's my chest, the rest is coming!" It set the others to giggling, and even Papa's lips twitched. But Mama's face remained unsmiling.

"Children, children!" she said earnestly. "Everyone has his own peculiar way of doing things. How do you know that we don't seem just as odd to Lena? You must learn to overlook different manners in people, because they don't matter. What is really important is whether the person has a good heart. This Lena has. More than that, she's very smart, and jolly besides. She's always ready to see the funny side, even in herself. I think she's a fine person! And last of all, if it weren't for her, we would have no little Charlie. Really, girls!"

The girls hung their heads and looked embarrassed.

"Well," Papa broke in, "I don't think the girls actually

intended to be mean about Lena."

"That's right, Mama," Henny said contritely. "I'm sorry. I didn't mean to sound nasty."

"We weren't very nice," Sarah apologized.

"We really like her an awful lot, Mama," said Charlotte earnestly.

"I know." Mama smiled at them reassuringly. "But sometimes we must think a little before we speak."

Into a dimly lit hallway and up three flights of stairs the family went. Aunt Rivka's tiny boxlike flat was already overflowing with old folks and young. Joyous greetings were exchanged. "Hello, hello!" "Happy Hanukkah!"

Gradually the grownups settled themselves near the big round table while the children were distributed on the couch, laps, assorted stools, and the floor. Someone started a song. With so much fun and laughter, others were encouraged to join. Someone else told a story, and soon the company vied with one another in telling amusing tales.

Aunt Rivka brought in the refreshments. There were high mounds of steaming latkes, fruit, nuts, raisins and dates, and finally her great specialty, rich, brown, moist slices of honey cake. Hot tea was poured into glasses for everyone.

All at once Uncle Solomon slapped his palm on the table.

63

"See, children!" he called out loudly. "See what I have!" He held up a leaden object which looked like a tiny alphabet block with a stem running right through its center. Each of its four sides bore a letter. "A dredel!" "A dredel!" the children cried.

Uncle Solomon smiled at them through his long white silky beard. "Whoever wants to play with the dredel must first tell what the letters are."

From various parts of the room there were shouts. "N, G, H, S!"

"That's all right," Uncle Solomon nodded his head. "But who can tell me what they stand for?"

An older boy stood up and recited in Hebrew, *"Nes Gadol Hayah Sham."*

"That's still all right," Uncle Solomon beamed. "But who knows what the words mean?"

And Ella answered proudly, her voice clear as a bell, "A great miracle happened there."

"Perfect!" Uncle Solomon handed the dredel to his son. "Here, Nathan, take the children into the kitchen and start them off. Aunt Rivka has the nuts all ready for you."

As the children trooped into the kitchen, there were wails from some of the smaller ones. "But we don't know how to play!"

"I'll teach you," Nathan said good-naturedly. "First, everyone sit down on the floor and make a circle." When everyone had done this, he continued. "Now we divide the nuts evenly amongst us. Then each puts his share in his own saucer. Now each one put a nut in the big bowl here in the center. Now watch." He gave the dredel a spin. "Let's see what letter comes up. You see, the letters also have a Jewish meaning." The dredel stopped. "Notice everybody, it's on the N. This stands for *nicht* or nothing. So I take no nuts from the big bowl." He turned to Henny. "Here, you spin next."

Henny gave the dredel a good hard turn, and it wobbled crazily till it stopped on G. "The G stands for *gantz*, meaning all. You're lucky. You get all the nuts in the bowl."

"But what do we do now, with no nuts left?" a little girl asked.

"Everybody has to put another nut into the bowl," Nathan replied. "Now the next person gets a chance to spin."

They played on. They soon learned that H stands for *halb*, half, which allows the player to take half the nuts from the bowl, and that S stands for *shtell*, or put, which means the player has to add another nut to the pile.

The children enjoyed the game immensely, and the afternoon just flew away. They didn't want to stop playing until Uncle Chaim uttered the magic words, "Hanukkah money! Come on, children!"

Thereupon the uncles and aunts made the rounds with a merry jingle of coins. "Happy Hanukkah!" they repeated over and over, as they dropped the precious pennies into open little palms.

And now parents began bundling up their little ones. It had grown late, and the party was at an end. Aunt Rivka and Uncle Chaim stood at the door bidding each one good-by. "May we always meet on happy occasions."

"It's so nice when relatives come together," Lena remarked when the family had assembled downstairs. "I'm glad Hyman brought me; I really enjoyed myself." She thrust a small parcel into Gertie's hands. "Here is my little Hanukkah present for all you girls."

"Oh!" "Oh!" Impatient fingers tore away the wrapping. The cover bounced off, and there, lined up in rows, were five shiny, satin sashes with five hair ribbons to match, in a rainbow array of colors. "Oh, Lena, they're lovely!" "Dear, dear Lena!" "You're so good to us!" Impulsively they hugged her and planted kisses on her round cheeks. All the while Uncle Hyman stood by, balancing from one leg to the other and grinning proudly.

When the hubbub had quieted down, he stepped forward. "And now we have something special for Charlie," he announced. He pulled out a big cigar and offered it to the little boy.

"Don't you think he's a little young for smoking?" Papa inquired jokingly, as Mama looked on somewhat concerned.

Charlie made a swift grab. The top of the cigar pulled out, releasing a tiny American flag in the shape of a fan. Everyone laughed as the astonished Charlie stared at the sudden change.

As Uncle Hyman and Lena waved good-by, Mama suddenly remembered something. "Oh, my! I left my umbrella!"

"I'll get it," Henny volunteered. She started back up the stairs.

"It's in the front room, by the window!" Mama shouted after her. "Ella, you wait for her," she said. "We'll go on ahead. It's way past Charlie's bedtime."

"Mama, can all of us girls wait so we can walk home together?" Sarah asked.

"All right. Ella, see they come right home."

Upstairs, as Henny picked up the umbrella, she glanced around the empty front room. It still bore traces of the recent gathering. On the partially cleared table was a large bowl of nuts. "Aunt Rivka," she called out, "can I have some nuts?"

"Why not?" Aunt Rivka shouted back from the kitchen. "Help yourself."

"How many can I take?"

She could hear Aunt Rivka laugh. "Take as much as you can carry."

Oh, boy, exclaimed Henny to herself. All I can carry! Her eyes were alight with sparks of mischief. Carefully she pushed the bowl towards the edge of the table. Pulling back several ribs of the umbrella, she tipped the bowl. In a moment, the nuts were cascading down in a rattle of sound.

As Henny sauntered past the kitchen on her way to the door,

she said smoothly, "Thank you, Aunt Rivka. You certainly let me take a lot."

Unsuspecting Aunt Rivka kept right on washing the dishes. "It's all right, my child," she replied, "the more, the merrier."

Henny spluttered with laughter. "Don't you want to see how many you gave me?" she asked mischievously.

Aunt Rivka picked up a towel for her soapy hands and stepped in to the front room. When she saw the empty nut bowl, her hands flew up in amazement. "How — why, Henny, you surely can't carry them all!" Henny held up the umbrella in triumph, and Aunt Rivka burst out laughing. "What a girl! Next time I'll know better than to give you such a chance, or I'll find myself with no house left."

"What's the matter with the umbrella?" Gertie asked in amazement as Henny came tramping out of the hallway. "It looks all blown up!"

Henny chuckled. "That's because it's full of something good!"

Charlotte pulled back a rib and peered inside. Her jaw dropped. "Ooh, nuts! Millions of 'em!"

Three more heads poked themselves inside. "Look out!" Henny yelled. "You'll break Mama's umbrella and spill out all my nuts!"

Ella turned on Henny. "Does Aunt Rivka know about this?"

"Certainly!" Henny countered. "And I was very polite, too. I asked her first."

"Do you expect me to believe that she actually let you have all these?"

Henny grinned. "She said to take as much as I could carry."

The grin widened from ear to ear. "So I only did what she told me."

"Mama won't like it," Sarah said immediately. "You know she always says when somebody offers you something, you're supposed to take just a little."

"It's all right. I showed Aunt Rivka how many I had, and she just laughed. I wanted to be sure there was enough for the five of us. Go on," Henny added generously, "help yourselves."

The girls fell to and soon shells were flying in all directions. The way homeward was slow, for every time one picked a butternut, she had to stop and stamp on it with her heel. After a few blocks Gertie observed, "The umbrella's getting skinnier and skinnier."

Charlotte turned back to stare at the litter of shells strewn behind them. "We're leaving a trail, just like Hansel and Gretel," she said.

By the time they reached their door, they were all full to bursting, and the little ones felt drowsy. "I'm so tired, my mouth is full of yawns," Gertie said.

Sarah stretched her arms wide. "I'm tired too. Didn't we have a good time, though? I wish every day was Hanukkah!"

Mad
and
Glad

THE WEEKLY WASH meant work for the whole family. On Saturday night when the sun had set and the Sabbath was over, Papa helped Mama with the washing. For hours they scrubbed away at the washboards. Then the clothes were boiled on top of the stove, in a large copper boiler. The kitchen had grown hot and steamy as Mama stirred and stirred the sudsy water with a well-worn wooden stick. She didn't stop till she was sure the clothes were really clean and sweet smelling. Because it was winter time, Papa had strung lines across the kitchen, and overnight the clothes dried.

Today was ironing day. The sprinkled clothes lay in neat rolls in a wicker basket. Papa had recently made a fine ironing board, and now it lay across the backs of two chairs. On it Mama was ironing all the hard-to-iron pieces like Papa's shirts and her own house dresses. Also the table became a huge ironing board, where Charlotte and Gertie ironed the handkerchiefs.

Henny sat on the couch mating pairs of stockings and socks. Ella and Sarah were folding large sheets and featherbed covers as Mama had taught them. Each held two corners of the large square. Flip, flap, they pulled it taut between them. Then, arms outstretched, they walked forward to meet each other, folding the smoothed sheet neatly in half. Again they took hold of opposite corners. Flip, flap. Flip, flap! Pull! This time it was folded in quarters. Now it was ready for the final ironing which they would give it later.

Charlie was busy, too. Bundled up in one of Mama's aprons, his little hands were splashing around in a toy washtub full of soapy water. Swish, swash, over and over, he kept washing the same bit of clothing. It seemed as if it never would be clean enough for him.

The door opened. "A regular laundry you got here," someone said admiringly.

"O my goodness, Lena! You here already? I didn't realize it was so late!" Mama glanced at the kitchen clock.

"Don't worry. You got plenty of time yet till supper. We stopped work early today; it's past the busy season. You don't mind I come so soon?" she added. "In my room, I'm only alone. It's quiet. Here is always children and laughing. It's homey."

"Mind! Why, it's a pleasure to have you, Lena."

"New dress?" Charlotte inquired, examining Lena's brown wool costume, which had a heavy braid design stitched onto the material. "It's pretty!"

"You like it? I made it myself. Think Hyman will like it? We're going out special tonight. To the theater on Second Avenue!"

"Of course he'll like it," Ella declared. "It's very becoming."

Lena smoothed the dress over her hips. "Makes me look not so fat, no?" she said. She looked around the room. "You're all so busy. Can I help, maybe?"

"Thank you, Lena," Mama replied. "You just sit down and be company. We're almost through, anyway."

Lena rocked back and forth on the rocking chair, keeping them all amused with her hearty chatter. From time to time, as the flatirons grew cold, Mama returned them to the stove, picking up freshly heated ones in their place. She'd wet her finger and swiftly strike the bottom of the iron. If it let out a pleasant *sizz-z-z,* she'd know it was hot enough for proper ironing.

By the time Papa arrived, the work was completed. The finished clothes were whisked away into closets and drawers, and the table was laid for supper. Only Uncle Hyman was missing.

74

"Everything will get all cold. Go ahead and eat," Lena urged. "Any minute now he'll be here. The way he eats, you don't have to worry. He'll catch up."

But supper was almost over before Uncle Hyman finally showed up, still wearing his working clothes. His suit was wrinkled and baggy. He had on an old shirt, frayed at the collar, and a day's whiskers had sprouted on his face. "Why so late?" Mama demanded.

"I couldn't help it. I was busy." Uncle Hyman scratched his ear. "Hello, children. Hello, Lena. My, you look nice!"

Lena frowned. "I certainly can't say the same for you!" she said in a huff. "Not enough you come late, so you look like a tramp!"

"Lena's right," Mama broke in. "Couldn't you have gone home first and changed?"

Uncle Hyman took off his cap and ran his fingers around the band. "It was too late to bother."

"Sure not! Why should you bother yourself getting all dressed up?" Lena fumed. "For you it's all right to take a girl to the theater looking like a *schlepper* so everybody should talk. I thought you were beginning to be different — to take care a little of yourself. But I made a big mistake. Once a *schlepper*, always a *schlepper!*"

75

As the torrent of words poured down on his disheveled head, Uncle Hyman turned red. His eyes sent appeals for help in Mama's direction, but Mama was on Lena's side. He sidled over to Lena and timidly put his hand on her shoulder. "Lena, please —" he muttered.

Lena wouldn't let him finish. "Keep away from me! You'll spoil my new dress!"

Uncle Hyman quickly hid the offending hand behind his back and swayed nervously from side to side.

The children felt uncomfortable. Yet somehow, it was like watching a play, wondering what would happen next. To Papa, it all seemed very amusing. He leaned way back in his chair, grinning broadly. But poor Mama was very distressed. Hand to cheek, she looked first at her brother and then at Lena.

"Listen, Lena." Uncle Hyman tried to speak mildly. "So you see me in my working clothes. Is that so terrible? After all, people should like each other for themselves and not —"

"According to you," Lena retorted hotly, "people should go around looking like pigs! How you belong to this family I don't know!" Her voice broke, and two big tears rolled down her cheeks. She picked up her coat from the leather couch. "You can go to the theater by yourself!" she flung at him, and flounced out of the house.

"Lena!" Uncle Hyman bellowed. Never before had the children seen him display such energy and speed. He yanked the door open and rushed to the stairs. "Please, Lena, wait!" His plea went unheeded. She was gone!

Slowly he shuffled back into the kitchen and stood by the window. His head drooped sadly. He stared down at the blanket of snow in the yard. After a moment they heard him say, "I'm so miserable. Honestly, I could throw myself out the window." He shivered and turned away. "Only it's too cold outside."

They wanted to laugh at his silly words, but he looked so woebegone that everyone felt sorry for him.

He sagged into a chair, his hands clasped. Nervously his thumbs circled round and round each other. "I should know it was so important!" he complained, all forlorn.

Mama threw up her hands. "What have I been telling you all these years?"

"Why don't you go after her and tell her you're sorry?" suggested Henny.

Uncle Hyman shook his head dolefully. "It won't help."

"Yes, it will," Ella replied. "Only you'll have to get fixed up first. When she sees you nice and clean, she'll change her mind."

"But it's so late already."

"If we all pitch in and help, you'll be in time." Ella jumped up excitedly. "Come on. Let's get started!"

"Come with me, Hyman," Papa said. "I'll see if I have a white shirt to lend you. Meanwhile you can wash and shave."

"A clean pair of socks also," Mama added.

"Quick, take off your shoes, Uncle Hyman," ordered Charlotte. "Gertie and I will polish them for you."

"I'll press your pants," Ella said.

Sarah ran around the kitchen busily. "I'm getting Papa's shaving things, and the brush and comb, and a clean towel!" she shouted.

"Mama, where's the whisk broom?" asked Henny. "So I can brush off his coat and cap."

At the sink, Mama stood over Uncle Hyman as if he were another one of her children. "Don't forget the ears! Maybe if you wash them out thoroughly, for once, you'll hear the things I tell you. And those nails! They look as if you've been planting potatoes!"

Uncle Hyman grunted and groaned at the sink while little Charlie added to the general hullabaloo by banging a spoon on the floor. "Wash! Wash! Wash!" he kept yelling.

The moment Uncle Hyman stepped away from the sink, Ella fell upon him with brush and comb. "Oh! Ouch!" he howled as the comb pulled at the tangles. Then she brushed the hair smooth till he winced. "Enough already!" he roared in exasperation. "My head is coming off!" With clever fingers, Ella pushed a wave into the dampened hair right above his forehead. "You'll see, Lena will be crazy about you now," Ella promised. "Girls like men with a wave in their hair."

"Yes, like Jules's hair," taunted Henny. "You can ride up and down on his waves."

At last Uncle Hyman was ready. "Some difference!" commented Papa. "Now at least you look like somebody."

"You think now she'll be satisfied?" Uncle Hyman asked hopefully.

"I'm sure she will," Mama said. "But you'd better hurry if you don't want to miss the show."

Quickly they helped him into his coat. He was about to pick up his old cap when Mama cried out, "Not that filthy thing! Papa, you lend him your derby."

The hat slipped down to rest on Uncle Hyman's ears. "I can't see a thing!" he exclaimed.

"Just a minute," Papa chuckled. "I can fix it." He rolled up a narrow piece of newspaper and tucked it inside the band. "Try it now."

"Fine. It fits." Uncle Hyman looked around gratefully. "Thank you — all of you and — and — children." He fumbled in his change pocket.

"Some other time," Mama put in quickly. "Go. Go!" and she shooed him gently out the door.

"Mama," Sarah suddenly remembered, "Uncle Hyman didn't have any supper!"

"Oh, my!" Mama cried. "We were so busy getting him fixed up, I forgot all about it!"

"Never mind, Mama," said Papa comfortingly. "Tonight he wouldn't even remember it himself."

It was past midnight, and the family was asleep. Suddenly there was a pounding on the kitchen door. Bang! Bang! Bang! "Open up! Open the door!" cried someone in the hall.

The children sprang from their beds in alarm, all except Gertie, who cowered underneath the covers.

"What's going on out there?" Papa shouted.

"It's me, Hyman! Lena and Hyman! Open the door! We want to see you!"

"Such crazy ones!" the children heard Papa mutter as he went toward the door. "They'll wake up the whole neighborhood!"

Behind him came Mama, looking like one of her own daughters with her hair in two long braids. The girls, in their nightgowns, stood in a tight circle around Papa, with timid Gertie holding on to Charlotte's hand. They peered inquisitively under Papa's arms as he unfastened the latch.

The door flew open. Lena and Uncle Hyman burst in, their faces joyful. "Don't be frightened. It's good news!" Lena cried. She stopped, remorseful. "Oh, my! The whole family we waked up! I'm sorry. We should have waited till tomorrow.

But we're so happy, we had to tell somebody right away."

Papa frowned impatiently. "Tell what?"

Hyman grabbed Papa's hand excitedly. "Feel my heart! It's jumping for joy! We're engaged!"

Lena exclaimed. "Just now it happened! Look — my engagement ring!"

"Really!" Mama heaved a happy sigh. "Well, that's just wonderful! Let me see the ring!"

"Let me! Me!" the children chimed in, with the younger ones flying around the room like nightgowned seagulls.

Roaring with laughter, Papa slapped Uncle Hyman heartily on his back. "Hyman, that I should live to see the day!"

"Lena, I'm so glad!" Mama exclaimed as she put her arms around her. "I couldn't have asked for anything better."

Lena hugged her in turn. "Before I was only alone. Now all at once, see what a big family I've got!"

"When will the wedding be?" inquired Ella.

"Will it be a big wedding?" Sarah broke in breathlessly. "In a hall like across the street?"

"Then you could wear a real wedding gown and everything," Charlotte said.

"Shush!" Lena answered. "Give us a chance. We haven't made up our minds yet."

No one noticed the little figure standing near the bedroom door, rubbing its eyes with its fists. "I waked up!" it peeped loudly for attention.

"Look who's here to join the party!" Papa cried, swinging his son to his shoulders. Charlie's mouth puckered into a puzzled smile. He gazed down on the ring of jolly faces below. "Party?" he repeated.

"Yes," chuckled Henny, "a nightgown party!"

"Tonight we celebrate!" Papa announced, waltzing around with Charlie. "Mama, bring the wine glasses!" From the kitchen closet he took out the decanter of wine reserved for special occasions. He poured the red wine into glasses, full to the brim for the grownups, just a thimbleful for each child. "Lena and Hyman, may this night mark the beginning of a wonderful life for both of you!" Papa said fervently. *"L'chaim* (to life)!" Glasses were raised high.

"L'chaim tovim (to a good life)!" was the rousing response, and everyone took a sip.

Lena finally set the third Sunday in June as the day for the wedding, and the family began to plan for the coming marriage. Uncle Hyman thought all this fuss unnecessary. "Why can't we go to the rabbi and let him marry us!" he wanted to know. Papa was inclined to agree.

But Mama and the girls all sided with Lena. "Don't you understand, Hyman," Lena said earnestly, "a wedding is the most important day in a girl's whole life! She wants it should be so wonderful, she should remember it forever!"

"Every girl dreams about it," Ella chimed in. "A beautiful wedding gown — a long white flowing veil — a bouquet of white

84

roses — music . . ." Her face wore a faraway look as if she were lost in her own dream.

But Papa was practical. "It's very nice, but big weddings cost a fortune."

Lena sighed. "I know. We've been finding that out. We'll have to be satisfied with something not so big — a ceremony in the synagogue, maybe." Her chin came up. "Never you mind, children. It'll still be a beautiful wedding, you'll see!"

Then one evening Lena came a-running in happy excitement. "It's all settled!" she cried. "We rented the hall across the street. Hyman is paying the deposit right now."

The children were beside themselves. They whooped and hollered with delight.

Mama was puzzled. "Lena, I don't understand — the money —" Just then Uncle Hyman came bustling in. "You can thank my brother Morris for this!" he exclaimed. "He's paying for the hall. It's his wedding present! And we have enough now to pay for everything else. How do you like that?"

"Really!" Mama's voice was full of pleased surprise. "Oh, Hyman, we have a good, good brother!"

"Yes," Uncle Hyman shook his head. "Now Lena can have a wedding with all the trimmings."

Ups
and
Downs

CHARLIE KEPT TUGGING at Mama's skirt. "Play with me," he implored.

"Mama's too busy now, Charlie." She brought out a box of empty spools which she had saved over the years. All of Mama's children had played with them. "Here, play by yourself."

Charlie always liked to play with the spools. He sat on his heels and built wobbly little houses, talking and singing to himself as he labored. No sooner were they up, than with one gleeful swoop of his arm, he'd send them tumbling down. After a while, he put one behind the other, and they became a long streetcar. "Clang! Clang!" the little conductor chanted as he crept along the kitchen floor.

Mama was glad she had found something to interest him. It was Friday, and she was busy with preparations for the Sabbath. The house to put in order, bread and cake to bake, the special Sabbath dinner to cook. She'd have to rush if she expected to be through in time.

It wasn't long, however, before Charlie was bored with his streetcar. He began kicking the spools with hands and feet, scrambling them all over the floor. The mixup seemed to please him, and he prattled away cheerily in his own baby language.

Mama kept stumbling over the rolling spools as she went back and forth. It made her cross. "Charlie, pick up the spools and put them back into the box!" she commanded.

Dutifully, Charlie started collecting the spools. It was a wonderful game, and he had lots of fun. He dived under the whatnot, inched his way in and out beneath the leather couch, and crawled under the table and chairs. He even poked into the coal box and rummaged through the open garbage pail. It took a long time, and when he was finished, he was a complete mess, his hands all grubby and his face smeared. He looked around. It was so quiet in the house. Where was everyone? "Mama," he asked, "where Dertie and Lotte?"

"In school," Mama answered shortly.

"I wanna go school," he said.

"You will when you get to be a big boy."

"I big boy now," he insisted.

Mama did not answer. She was kneading her challis dough.

It had risen beautifully, nice and spongy. It would make two fine loaves. She nodded with satisfaction.

Charlie climbed up on a chair so he could watch Mama. How different things looked up here! He looked on, spellbound, while Mama's swift hands pushed the soft mass of dough on the bread board. In and out and round about the hands went. Schwiggle schwaggle! In the bread pan right before him lay another big lump, just like Mama's. He poked it lightly with an exploring finger. It made a nice little hole, but in a moment, the hole seemed to fill up. He poked it again. Such a nice mushy feeling! He pulled at it with both hands trying to imitate Mama's kneading motions. "Mama, see!" he exulted. Mama saw and let out a cry of distress. "Oh, Charlie! With your dirty hands!"

"Dirty hands?" He opened his little fists and examined them curiously. He rubbed them against the sides of his rompers, and held them up to view. "Clean!" he smiled.

Quickly Mama rescued the dough and cut away the dirty part. "Look what you did!" she kept saying. "Tsk, tsk!" With a practiced eye she measured the remainder. "It'll never be enough now!"

Charlie didn't understand. Why was Mama's face all scowly, her voice so angry? I wanna schwiggle, schwaggle like

88

Mama, he thought to himself, and Mama's angry. He didn't like it here any more. He pushed his lips forward in a pout. "Go see Mr. Basch."

"Good! Then I'll be able to get my work done." Mama shook her finger at him sternly. "Remember! You're not to go outside! You go to Mr. Basch's store through the back door."

Mama stood watching at the landing as he plodded down the stairs. Both hands tightly gripping the balusters, he sidled down with one foot, the other following closely behind. As he disappeared through the back way, Mama sighed with relief and hurried back to her work.

The store was empty of customers. Mr. Basch was sitting in a chair propped up against the counter reading a newspaper. He glanced up. "Hello, Charlie, my friend! Shake hands!" Solemnly the little boy offered his hand. "My Mama don't smile on me," he said.

"Hmmm." Mr. Basch peered down over his glasses into the cracker barrel. He bent down and picked out two pieces of broken lemon snaps. He offered one to Charlie, and they munched together in silence.

When the cracker was all gone, Charlie went through Mr. Basch's back door and clambered up the long flight of stairs into the family kitchen. Mama was at the stove. Charlie walked over and said not a word. He just stood and stared up at her.

Mama was sampling her soup. Charlie could see that her face wore a frown. Without even looking at him, she said, "You back already? Keep away from the stove!"

All Charlie heard was "keep away!" He turned right around and walked out. Down the stairs he went, back into the store straight to where Mr. Basch was sitting. "My Mama don't smile on me," he said cheerlessly.

Mr. Basch put down his paper. Thoughtfully he stroked his beard. Once again his arm went into the barrel and up came the broken pieces. Mr. Basch examined them carefully. "Chocolate snaps, I think, Charlie." Again they nibbled away without speaking. Then Mr. Basch said, "I tell you what, Charlie. You go upstairs and tell Mama you'll be a good boy and see what happens."

So once again Charlie went through the door and started the toilsome journey up the staircase and into the kitchen.

Mama's work was going very well. She was humming a little tune. Hands on hips she turned around and studied the small boy. All her babies had been adorable, she thought, but this one, he was such a little love of a man. My goodness, such a serious expression on his sweet face. She smiled.

Charlie rushed into the hall and plodded down the stairs

to where he knew Mr. Basch was waiting. "My Mama smiles on me!" he exclaimed. Without waiting for an answer, he about-faced and climbed right up the stairs again.

Mama found all this coming and going highly amusing. When Charlie planted himself in front of her and gazed questioningly upward, she gave him a great, big smile.

Down the stairs again went Charlie to his friend Mr. Basch. "My Mama smiles another time!" he cried gleefully.

"Well, that's fine, Charlie — very, very fine!" Mr. Basch grinned. Somehow he too felt as lighthearted as the little boy. He nodded his head understandingly as he watched Charlie run through the door again.

When Charlie came back to Mama, she nearly doubled over with laughter. Charlie ran over and buried his head in her skirts. He felt so good!

Laughter bubbled up inside him too. He threw back his little head and laughed and laughed and laughed.

Queen of the May

"I wonder who'll make a May party this year," said Gertie.

"I don't know. Nobody asked me to join any yet," Charlotte replied.

"We ought to make one ourselves," Henny suggested.

"That's a marvelous idea!" Sarah cried enthusiastically. "With Ella in charge, it would be the fanciest May party anybody ever saw!"

"Thanks," Ella answered, "but do you realize how much work a May party is?"

"We could all help," Sarah said coaxingly.

"Well —" Ella hesitated. The sisters could tell the idea was catching on. "It would be a lot of fun."

Charlotte clapped her hands together. "Oh, Ella, who'll be the Queen? Who'll be the Queen of the May?"

Gertie jumped up and down. "Ooh! I want to be the Queen!"

"I'm sorry," Ella told them, "but you're too little to be Queen, both of you."

Their disappointment lasted only a moment, for by now Ella's imagination was running riot. "Gertie, you could be a little green elf with a peaked cap. And I'll twist strips of green and brown crepe paper for a belt. You'd be the cutest thing!"

"If I can't be Queen, could I be a fairy, Ella?" Charlotte burst in. "With big silver wings on my back? I'd like that!"

"Yes," Ella considered. "A silver band on your head, maybe. It would look nice against your brown hair."

"I guess Henny ought to be Queen," Sarah said resignedly. "With her curls and all."

"Not me," Henny replied quickly. "I'm much too grown up. I'll help Ella with the managing. Why don't you be the Queen, Sarah?"

"But maybe one of the other girls who join up will want to be the Queen."

"Since we're making it, I think it's only fair that somebody in our family should be Queen."

"Besides," Ella continued, "there are all kinds of other wonderful things they could be."

And that's how Sarah got to be Queen of the May.

The ten days that followed were filled with activity. The

children combed the neighborhood. "Want to join our May Party?" they asked friends and relatives. "It costs only ten cents to pay for the costumes."

Ella kept strict account of the money that came in, and soon she was able to report that they already had twenty dimes. "Wow!" exclaimed Gertie, "twenty children! And don't forget there's us, too!"

"Yes," said Ella. "I think that ought to be enough. Let's not ask anybody else. We'll have an awful lot to do as it is."

Every afternoon, Mama's kitchen seemed to burst at the seams with children of the neighborhood. Children of all shapes and sizes stopped by for fittings and remained to cut and twist, pin and stitch, color and paste, all under artist Ella's direction. Crowns and wings and flowers, hats and wands and belts, rapidly came into being. It was just as Mama said, "Many hands make work light."

Some of the other mamas pitched in too. Even Lena took to dropping in evenings to lend an expert sewing hand.

Papa went to work with his carpenter tools and fashioned a Maypole. It had a broomstick handle for the pole and a wooden hoop from a sugar barrel for its wheel-like top. Ella wound strips of white, pink, and blue paper around the pole and criss-crossed them over the hoop. Next many colored streamers and dainty flower rosettes were hung from it. When at last Ella had finished, everyone agreed it was a miracle of loveliness.

The night before, everything was ready. "There," Ella said with satisfaction as she twisted the last leaf into the garland of flowers for Queen Sarah's head. "Try it on, Sarah." She eyed her thoughtfully. "It doesn't look right with braids. You'll have to wear your hair loose tomorrow."

"I know," agreed Sarah. "It has to be loose. If only it was curly like Henny's," she added wishfully.

Lena spoke up. "If Mama says it's all right, I could make you lovely curls first thing in the morning. I just bought a marvelous curling iron!"

"But doesn't it hurt the hair?" Mama asked doubtfully.

"No. You just have to be a little careful. Don't worry. I know how to use it. Sarah will have curls just as nice as Henny's, you'll see."

The eventful day dawned, blue-skied, sunny, and warm. Lena arrived bright and early with the curling iron, and the family gathered around to watch as she went to work. First she lit the gas stove and thrust the long iron into the blue flame. In a few moments she pulled it out, testing its heat by twirling it swiftly in the air. "Now, Sarah," she cautioned, "stand perfectly still." *Hiss-s-s!* the iron steamed as Lena skillfully wound a small bunch of Sarah's hair over and over up towards the scalp, Sarah held her breath. Would it really make a curl? Now slowly, carefully the hair was being unwound.

There it was — a long, thick, perfect curl! "Oh, Sarah, it's just gorgeous!" Charlotte cried. Sarah's fingers reached up timidly as if fearful that the magic curl would disappear at her touch. It was true! It was real! Round and smooth and shapely. "Oh, Lena! Let's hurry and do the rest!"

When it was over, Sarah raced to the bedroom mirror. She stared at herself. Was this stranger Sarah? Slowly she turned her head, studying herself from all angles. Lena put a mirror in her hand so she could see the back of her head as well. It was thrilling to feel the long blonde curls bob against her cheeks, her shoulders, her back! Starry-eyed, she threw her arms around Lena. "Thanks a million, billion times!"

Henny was mystified. "Such a fuss about curly hair! Wait till tomorrow when it'll be all tangled up. You won't be so over-joyed then when you have to comb and brush it out."

Right after lunch, Ella jumped up and clapped her hands. "Listen, everybody. Now's the time! Get dressed, and we'll meet the others downstairs."

"That's right," Mama approved. "If they all come tramping in here, it'll be a madhouse."

Such a flurry and to-do! But everything went according to plan. Soon the Queen, followed by a dazzling fairy and a quaint elf, was standing impatiently in front of the house. Charlie was there too, dressed as a small Uncle Sam in red, white, and blue, with a cardboard hat tilted rakishly on his head.

Now other fairy-book folk appeared. There was Red Riding Hood approaching, hand in hand with Little Boy Blue. Here came a red devil and a scary witch in black. Close behind followed a little Dutch girl in white cap and apron with a blond Dutch boy for her partner. Soon the street was a-sparkle with all the colors of the rainbow.

Ella cupped her hands. "Line up, everybody!" she shouted. Two by two the children fell into place, with Queen Sarah standing proudly at their head. As she held the beribboned May-pole aloft, her curls caught the gold of the afternoon sun. Lena turned to Mama with a smile. "With such curls, she feels like a real Queen."

Henny ran up and down the line to see if everything was in order. "Forward, march!" Ella gave the command. The glittering array moved down the street, past the crowd of admiring spectators. At the very end of the line rolled several gaily decorated carts containing the smallest children. Last of all came Charlie. He stood up in his red, white, and blue wagon waving with his cane at the curious little outsiders who trotted along behind.

"Sit down!" Henny ordered, "or you'll fall!"

They were about halfway to the park when a gray patch of cloud fell across the sun. A sudden gust of wind set costumes rustling. Anxiously Ella scanned the sky. It grew darker. The wind rose, scattering dust and papers before it. The Maypole swayed back perilously. Sarah had to hold on with all her might. There was a rumble of thunder, and a few blobs of rain spattered the marchers. "My costume will get all melted!" a little girl lamented. The drops grew heavier.

"Oh, how awful!" Henny cried despairingly. "Ella, what'll we do?"

Ella stood still, thinking hard. Then it came to her. She knew what to do. Her arm shot forward. "This way, everybody. Turn left!" she shouted. "Double quick time! One, two — one, two!"

In less time than it takes to tell, the whole parade, Maypole, carts, children, and all, had disappeared into Papa's shop. Just in the nick of time, too! Cr-a-ack! A sharp clap of thunder bounced over the rooftops, and the rain pelted down in torrents.

Papa was in the back making up a rag bale when the army of youngsters swooped down upon him. He jumped out of the bin and came running. "What's this?" he shouted above the din.

"It started raining, and we were nearby. And I had to save the costumes!" explained Ella.

"Raining! Oh, my!" Papa passed his fingers through his hair. All about him were long faces. "It's really a shame," he said sympathetically.

"The grounds will be all soaking and full of puddles!" Queen Sarah was close to tears.

"And we were going to dance around the Maypole and everything," Gertie said, whimpering. In another second, the other smaller children had joined in, loudly wailing their disappointment.

"Stop yammering!" Ella yelled. "We can still have our May Party. We'll have it right here. That is —" she turned questioningly — "if it's all right with my papa."

Ella could see that Papa wasn't exactly pleased. But with a host of little boys and girls staring up at him pleadingly, he just couldn't say no. "Well, what with the rain, there won't be any business. The peddlers will be coming in anyway, so I couldn't do much work." A grin was slowly spreading across his face as if he too were being caught up by the party spirit. "Come on, Queen Sarah! On your throne!" He lifted her up in his strong arms and perched her high on his rolltop desk.

Pulling off the lid of the empty pot bellied stove, he stuck the Maypole inside. It looked so comical there, the children shrieked with laughter. "The stove's got an umbrella!" a little boy cried.

"Clear the center!" Ella called out. She and Henny pulled the chairs away from the stove and backed them up against the walls. Papa brought out boxes, old newspaper bundles, and piles of rag sacks. "Sit down, everybody!" ordered Ella, and there was a mad scramble for places.

No sooner was everyone seated than the peddlers came straggling in. All wet and bedraggled, they stared around bewilderedly. "Say, Pop, you make the school?" peddler Joe wanted to know.

"Join the party!" everyone greeted the newcomers.

"But I ain't dressed up!" Picklenose moaned with comical sadness. A little boy ran forward and yielded up a gold paper crown. Picklenose promptly balanced it on the top of his head. "Don't I look fancy?" he exclaimed, swaggering up and down.

Ella struck up a song. "Today's the first of May, May, May! Today's the first of May!" coaxing everyone to join. Joe pulled out a battered harmonica from a pocket and played along. The air was filled with music as one rousing tune followed another with different youngsters standing up to lead.

Then Scotty took the center of the floor. "Watch this kids!" he roared. He danced a lively sailor's hornpipe. The delighted children clapped their hands and beat out the rhythm with their feet. When the dance was over, they clamored for more. Scotty was puffing hard and mopping his brow. "I guess I ain't as spry as I used to be," he apologized. "So, with your Highness's permission, Queen Sarah, I'd like to sit me down."

Polack made a face. "Bah! You call that a dance! I show you real dance — Polish dance. Joe, you play the song — you know — the one I already teach you." He grabbed hold of

Henny's arm and began to hop and leap about, yelling out the steps to her. The pair turned and twisted and flew all around the basement as the children screamed with delight. The dance ended with Polack twirling Henny high in the air. "Now that's what I call a dance!" he said proudly, as he bowed to the loud applause.

Now Queen Sarah clapped her hands. "Ladies of my court, let the Maypole dance begin!"

Picklenose jumped up eagerly. "Seeing as I still got my crown on, I'll hold the Maypole." He lifted it high. The bigger girls formed a circle and took hold of the streamers. In and out and under they waltzed, winding the ribbons in pretty patterns around the pole. This time it was the peddlers who did the applauding. They stamped their feet and whistled.

Charlotte sprang on a chair. "Listen, everybody!" she cried, "why don't we have a play, especially since we're all wearing costumes!"

Everyone was enraptured with the idea. "Tell us a story, Charlotte. Then we can act it out," they cried. The room grew quiet as Charlotte began to make up a play. But she didn't get very far. Every head turned towards the staircase. A very wet pair of shoes was squeaking, squidge, squidge, squidge down the steps.

"So this is where you are," an excited voice hailed them. It was Uncle Hyman, all soaked and dripping. "I was running all over the park looking for you! He waved his hands at them. "Now, please, everybody, don't get lost again. Wait right here till I come back! Loudly the shoes squidged up the stairs again, leaving a wet trail behind them.

Papa shrugged his shoulders. "Where's that *meshugener* (crazy one) going?"

"Go on with the play, Charlotte," urged one of the elves.

Charlotte considered a moment. "Well, now let's see. Where was I. Oh —."

The squidgy sounds were heard again, only slower this time. Uncle Hyman appeared, arms laden with two bulging paper bags. He staggered over to Sarah and set the bags down on the desk. "See what I got!"

The youngsters bounded out of their seats and milled around the Queen. Sarah thrust her hand inside one of the bags and came up with something. With a big smile, she held it up for all to see. There was a tremendous shout. "Ice cream sandwiches!" A forest of eager hands stretched forward to receive the surprise. "Gimme one!" "Gimme one!" Six active hands popped furiously in and out of the bags as Henny and Ella rushed to Sarah's rescue. Luckily there was enough for everyone, including the peddlers. As the youngsters bit into the crisp cracker covering, a boy cried out, "Gee, this is the best part of all. Thanks a lot, Mr. Uncle."

That reminded the others of their manners, and thank-yous for Uncle Hyman came flying from every side.

You could see Uncle Hyman was pleased, but he waved his hands to shush them. "So stop thanking me already and eat," he spluttered. "The ice cream will melt."

A golden shaft of light suddenly spread across the cellar steps. "Look, the sun's out!" someone cried.

"Now it shines," observed Papa. "Just when the party's over."

"Well, at least we'll be able to march back without spoiling our costumes," Ella declared. "Line up, all of you, as we were in the beginning."

There was a hustle and bustle. Then, like a dazzling rainbow, the column of masqueraders filed up the stairs and out into the sunshine.

"Did you ever hear of a May Party in a cellar?" the witch said to Puss-in-Boots.

"I'm glad it rained!" exclaimed little Bo-Peep. "It was the best May Party ever."

And everyone agreed.

Eight
at
One Blow

THE WEDDING was only six weeks away. Uncle Joe had given Mama material for the girls' dresses — yards of the daintiest French voile with plenty of lace for trimming. Mama's sewing machine whirled constantly as she and Lena took turns with the dressmaking.

Fittings were exciting but tiresome too. Lena pinned and marked and pinned again. Sarah said it made her feel faint to have to stand still for so long. But when the pieces of material actually began to look like dresses, the girls were thrilled.

"What's Charlie going to wear, Mama?" Gertie asked.

"A little black velvet suit with a white collar. Lena and I have it all planned."

"Oh, he'll look so cute! Just like Little Lord Fauntleroy!" exclaimed Charlotte.

"I hope you girls appreciate how much Lena is helping," Mama commented. "Especially when she's so busy too."

"We certainly do," Ella replied warmly. "Lena, you're an angel! Here you are, working so hard on our things, and you haven't even started on your own dress yet."

Lena smiled. "My dress is nearly finished."

"It is? But how, when?"

"Every day I come to work early. Before the others. The boss lets me use the electric machine. It goes very fast that way."

"What's the dress like, Lena?" the girls questioned.

"You'll see it at the wedding." And no matter how much they wheedled and begged, that's all Lena would say.

The last week in May came riding in on an unexpected wave of heat. The city was like a giant oven, the air close and heavy. Swarms of flies appeared everywhere. They lit on the piles of refuse and the open garbage cans in the streets, feasting greedily. They zoomed in through the windows and buzzed annoyingly about the rooms. To clear the house, Mama laid sheets of sticky fly paper on the window ledges and on the table, and hung several long curly strips of it from the ceiling. Papa brought home a fly swatter, and the children fought for a chance to slap away at the pests.

"Oh, dear," Mama said, wiping the perspiration from her forehead. "If it's so hot now, what's it going to be like when it's really summer?"

"Hotter," Henny answered promptly.

"I bet it's real cool on the beach," Sarah sighed. "I wish we could live at the seashore for the whole summer."

"Yes," agreed Ella. "We ought to get away from the city for once!" But she was sorry she had said that, for she noticed the troubled look on Mama's face. She knew Mama wished they could too.

"I'm going with my friends to the river dock right after lunch," Henny broke in. "How about lending me your pink blouse, Ella?"

"But I haven't even worn it myself yet," Ella answered.

"What are you saving it for? What's the sense in having pretty clothes if you just let them hang in the closet?"

"You mean I'm supposed to rush right away and put on something new the minute I get it, the way you do? No, thanks. I was saving it."

"Oh, come on," Henny urged. "We can wash and iron it before your next date with that Julius."

Ella flushed. "Never you mind about Jules! You know very well after you get through with any of my things they look like rags."

"Please, Ella! I'll be extra careful this time, I promise!"

"All right. But remember, if there's so much as a single

button loose, I'll never lend you anything again!"

"Gee, thanks." Henny skipped off to the bedroom to put on her borrowed finery.

For lunch Mama set a platter of cold homemade corned beef and boiled potatoes on the table. "This certainly looks good," Papa said, "but where's the pickle?"

"Oh, my!" exclaimed Mama. "I forgot! And pickle goes so good with corned beef, too."

"So how long would it take to get some?" Papa demanded. "The stand's just around the corner." He turned to Charlotte. "Would you like to go?"

"Yes, Papa." Charlotte pushed back her chair and started towards the door. On the way, she bumped into the long wire handle of the fly swatter lying on the washtub. Absent-mindedly she picked it up and carried it along as she skipped down the stairs. She flipped it back and forth enjoying the pleasant little swishing sound it made.

She reached the corner. My, but the sun was hot! She walked close to the buildings, where the fire escapes made small islands of shade on the sidewalk. A garbage can blocked her path. "Wow, look at all those flies!" she exclaimed. She watched them circling over the rim. Fascinated, she stood quite still as they hovered, settled, and ate their fill. She waved the fly swatter threateningly, and a host of insects flew off to cling to the nearby wall.

Wouldn't it be marvelous if people could walk on a wall like that, she thought. Or upside down on the ceiling! Things would look awful funny when you saw them upside down. Of course I wouldn't want to be a fly. Nobody likes them. Still it would be fun to go flying around. How can they hang on the way they do? Do they have glue on their feet?

She tried to imagine what it would feel like to have gluey feet. Stretching her arms wide as if they were wings, she flapped them up and down, keeping her feet tight to the sidewalk. She didn't like being stuck. One foot at a time, she pulled her feet out of the glue with a great deal of effort, till at last she was free.

She brushed the wall idly with her swatter, and the flies scattered. One particularly bold one came to roost right on top of her straight little nose. It tickled. She shooed him away. Why, there was a fly swatter in her hand. She had almost forgotten. Slowly she raised it, bringing it down with a hard smack against the wall. Several flies fell to the ground.

Suddenly a new thought struck her. Was it mean to kill flies? She held the swatter still. Teacher said they carry germs and make people sick. They land on your food right from the garbage cans and dirt. Even if you chased them away, the germs still stayed. And then you ate them up with the food you put in your mouth. "Ugh!" Charlotte shivered in disgust. "I'm not going to eat any more of your old germs!" Whack! Whack! She laid about with the swatter furiously.

She stopped for a moment to let them collect again. How many could she catch at one time? In the fairy story, the tailor killed seven at one blow! She sneaked up on tiptoe and slammed the swatter against the wall with a mighty wallop. "There!" she panted triumphantly as she counted the slain enemy. Her face lengthened in disappointment. "Only three," she muttered. "You nasty old creatures! I'm going to keep right on swatting away till I smash even more than the tailor."

All this time the family sat around the table waiting impatiently for Charlotte and the pickles. Papa glanced at Mama. "Where in Heaven's name could she have gone just for some pickle?" he growled.

"Maybe she got lost," Gertie said.

"Lost! Just around the corner!"

Mama was puzzled. "I wonder what's keeping her?"

Everyone stared hungrily at the meat laid out in neat slices on their plates. "I think I'll just take a small snip for a taste," declared Henny.

"Me, too," Gertie echoed.

Pretty soon all the girls were snatching "tastes," till Mama said, "Well, we might as well eat. I'm sure she'll be here any minute."

They all fell to. When the meat and potatoes had disappeared, they started on their fruit compote and drank their tea. Still no Charlotte!

They cleared the table, leaving a place set for the missing one. Mama turned to Ella with an anxious frown. "I think you'd better go see what —" Just then in came Charlotte. Triumphantly she held up the fly swatter. "Ha, ha! Eight at one blow!" she whooped.

"Nice time to come with the pickles!" Mama exclaimed. "And where are they?"

Charlotte gazed up at her. Suddenly she remembered. "Oh!" Slowly she put the fly swatter back on the washtub. Taking the pickle money out of her apron pocket, she handed it back to Mama without a word.

"Charlotte, Charlotte, when are you ever going to wake up?" Papa cried in despair.

But Mama only said, "Sit down, child, and finish your dinner."

"Without pickle," giggled Henny.

Everyone laughed. Even Charlotte.

Epidemic in the City

JUNE ARRIVED. In three weeks, the wedding would take place. Everything was ready. Uncle Hyman had even put down a deposit on a tiny three-room apartment in the Bronx.

"So far away!" the children wailed when they first heard about it.

Mama felt sad. "We'll miss you," she said.

"How far is it?" Lena replied. "A person would think I was going to Africa. It's only a subway ride. You should see how nice it is up there. Wide streets, and so new! It even smells new. My apartment is in a big modern building. But mostly it's still two-family houses with a little garden in the back. And on the block — trees!"

"Trees! In the streets!"

"Lots of people are moving away from the East Side," Mama remarked. "Still, we shouldn't complain. Our home is comfortable. Better than most."

Every spare moment Lena and Uncle Hyman went in and out of the furniture stores on Avenue A, examining and bargaining. Sometimes they took the girls along. "Fixing up a real home is much more fun than a make-believe one," Sarah said to Ella.

Now trouble appeared on the horizon. It hung like an evil cloud over the city. Everywhere people spoke of it in fear. Infantile paralysis! The terrible disease was occurring all over the city, crippling and destroying little children.

Regularly each summer the disease had made its appearance, but never before had so many been struck down. In this year of 1916, it had turned into an epidemic. Their faces gray with worry and fright, parents whispered to one another: Epidemic! The newspapers printed it in bold black headlines: Epidemic!

Like so many other mothers, Mama sewed up six little cloth bags and filled them with squares of Japanese camphor. "They say if you wear camphor, it keeps the germs away," she explained to the children.

So, day in and day out, the children wore the little bags next to their skin. Dangling from a string around their necks, the bag bounced up and down with every move. At first the children found the odor unbearable, but gradually they grew accustomed to it. Only Charlie kept tugging at the string till the bag ripped off. "Don't like the funny smell," he would cry petulantly. Mama finally had to pin the bag to his undershirt where he couldn't get at it.

Soon there were empty seats in the classrooms, and the clang of the ambulance bell was heard more and more frequently. Each night Mama prayed for the little ones that had been taken away. She also asked God that her own family might be spared.

Then the blow fell! No — not Mama's children. Nor any of the relatives' children. It was Lena who was stricken!

"Lena, a grown woman! How is it possible?" Mama asked. "Infantile paralysis is a children's disease!"

It happened three days before the wedding. Everything came to a sudden halt. Mama put the shining wedding dresses away in the girls' closet, where they hung desolately. Papa insisted Uncle Hyman stay with them. Like a wandering ghost, he plodded back and forth from the hospital to the house, his face pale, his hair all matted on his forehead, and his eyes red-rimmed.

The girls were heartsick. How they wished there was something they could do. Every evening when Papa came home, first thing, he'd ask, "How is she?" Uncle Hyman would only shake his head in silence. The pain inside him was too big for words.

Finally, after all the anxious waiting, there was the happy day when Mama and Uncle Hyman came back from a talk with the doctor. "Lena's going to be all right. The doctor says she was lucky."

"Thank God!" sighed Papa. He drew out his handkerchief and blew his nose.

The days passed, and the plague continued to mount. Mama kept refilling the camphor bags, even though by now she had little faith in them. All over the East Side the frightened people were leaving their homes. All they wanted was to get away. Away somewhere, anywhere, where the air would be clean. Each morning saw neighbors pile their belongings on wagons with the children safely settled on top. Mama and the girls watched wistfully as the wagons slowly clip-clopped away.

One night Mama said. "Papa, I met a woman in the butcher shop today. She's going out to Rockaway Beach for the rest of the summer. She told me they still have one more place left to rent out."

"It must cost quite a lot of money," Papa said thoughtfully.

Quickly Mama replied. "No. She said it was very reasonable at this place. Oh, Papa — what do you think?"

"I think, Mama, that you should go right out there tomorrow and put down a deposit," Papa said firmly.

At dawn the next day, Mama left for Rockaway Beach, while Ella kept house and looked after the family. Towards evening, when a weary Mama returned, the girls could tell at once that it was good news she brought. "Well, children," she said with a smile, "it's all settled! We're going to the seashore!"

"Honest?" "Oh, Mama, how marvelous!" The children were thrilled.

"Just think! We can go bathing every single day!" Charlotte exclaimed.

"And play in the sand!" Gertie added. "Charlie will just love it! He's never even seen a beach!"

Ella took hold of Mama's hand. "For the first time in our whole lives," she said, "we're all going away on a vacation! The whole family!"

"We have Papa to thank," Mama reminded them. "He will have to work extra hard to pay for this."

Immediately the girls tumbled all over their Papa, hugging him hard.

"All right, all right! Enough already!" Papa shook them off good-naturedly.

"It won't be much of a vacation for Papa," Mama remarked sadly. "It's too far for him to come out every night."

Never before had the family been separated — not even for

a day. "You mean," Sarah asked tearfully, "we're not going to see Papa the whole summer?"

"Don't worry. You'll see me," Papa reassured her. "Every Friday I'll close the shop early and come out. You'll be having such a good time the whole week long, before you know it, it'll be Friday."

Ella was worried about Papa. "But who'll clean up the house? And who'll make your meals when Mama's away?"

"Aw," Henny waved her hand, "let the house stay dirty. We'll clean it up when we get back. And Pop's a good cook."

"I certainly am." Papa smiled at her. "I'm a first class cook. Ask Mama. When we first got married, I had to teach her how to make *gefüllte* fish and even how to clean a chicken."

"I suppose that's true," Mama replied, laughing. "Anyway, it makes a good story."

The children woke that first morning with a sense of strangeness. Ella held up her finger. "Listen," she said. There was no sound of pushcarts, nor wagons, nor streetcars. Instead they could hear a constant rattling of the windows as if some giant were huffing and puffing on them. From a distance came the dull swish of the surf pounding and breaking on the shore.

"I can't wait to get into that ocean," exclaimed Henny.

"Me, too," the others echoed.

Springing from their beds they fairly flew through breakfast and the household chores. Then they put on their bathing suits. "Now children, be very careful," Mama cautioned. "The water here is much rougher than at Coney Island. Ella, you watch them, especially Charlie."

"Aren't you coming with us, Mama?"

"Not this morning. Too much to do. I'll go with you in the afternoon. Run along and enjoy yourselves."

They clattered down a flight of wooden stairs and onto the front porch. Comfortable rocking chairs invited them to sit down and gaze out on the wide sunny street, with its two-story houses hedged in by shrubbery. A fitful wind blew through the leaves of the trees that lined the curb. "Isn't it just lovely!" Charlotte murmured.

Sarah drew a deep breath of air into her lungs. "It smells sort of salty, doesn't it?" she observed.

"Yes," Ella replied. "I can hardly believe it was just yesterday we were in the hot city."

When they got to the beach, Charlie stared at the onrushing ocean with eyes big as saucers. "Pick me up!" he pleaded. He cuddled close to his big sister, every so often peeping out warily at the unfamiliar surroundings.

Ella carried him down to the water's edge, but she could not make him go in. It did no good to say, "Don't be scared, Charlie. See, all the little boys and girls are playing in the water." To Charlie, the white-capped waves seemed like a big angry monster hurtling forward to snatch him up and carry him away — away out there, into the deep green beyond. The noise was deafening. He screamed, turned his back on the dreadful thing, and fought to get away. He tried to run across the sand, but his bare little feet had nothing to grip under him. He slipped and fell. Hiding his head in his arms, he bawled pitifully as his sisters hastened to his rescue.

Ella sat down and took him in her lap. She rocked him in her arms, speaking soothingly all the while. "All right, Charlie, don't cry. You don't have to go in if you don't want to. Nobody's going to make you."

The sisters were sorry. They had been so sure Charlie would like the beach as much as they did. "But he's never even seen the ocean before," Ella explained to them. "We have to give him time to get used to it. Go in without me. I'll stay with Charlie. But mind, not too far out!"

When Charlie's tears ceased to flow at last, Ella gathered some large seashells. Together they scooped out tunnels in the clean white sand. She brought water, and they made mud pies.

Soon Charlie began to feel at home with the sand, creeping around happily on his hands and knees. He liked the feel of the wet sand squidging through his fingers and toes. Gradually they moved closer and closer to the water's edge without his even realizing it. He was busily digging a hole, when a wave, bolder than its companions, rolled right up under him. Like a jack

rabbit, Charlie scooted away, but he wasn't much frightened any more. He laughed aloud. "It tickles!" he cried to Ella.

When Friday arrived, the family felt glad because Papa was coming. In the late afternoon they all walked to the railway station to meet him.

Papa seemed pale compared to the sunburnt countenances around him. But it was good to see his familiar face light up the moment he spied them. He kissed each one in hearty greeting. "My, how marvelous you all look! Such rosy cheeks and such clear and shining eyes! Mama, they're just blooming!"

Mama laughed gayly. "It's the bathing and fresh air. It gives them a wonderful appetite. I can't seem to give them enough to eat."

"And you should see all the milk we drink out here!" Charlotte chimed in. "Mama says we ought to have our own cow."

That night they attended services at the temple nearby. It was a big, important-looking building, altogether different from Papa's tiny synagogue on the East Side. In the city only Papa went on Fridays to pray, before the evening meal. Here Papa could do that, too, but after supper, everybody went to temple — men, women, and children. And they all sat together!

Ella could tell Papa felt a little strange. She could see he missed the friendly atmosphere of his own synagogue where everyone chanted aloud in Hebrew, in his own fashion. In this grand temple, services were formal. The congregation sat listening quietly while the rabbi preached a sermon, mostly in English, in a resounding voice. "Just like an actor," Ella whispered.

"Praying in English!" Papa sniffed. "Some rabbi! He hasn't even got a beard."

But the girls liked the services. They enjoyed listening to the choir and joining in the communal reading from the prayer books. If I could only be in a choir like that, Ella thought.

As they walked home, Mama linked her arm through Papa's. "Well, Papa, I guess the world has to move on. New times — new ways!"

"I suppose it's all right," Papa answered. "They have good

Jewish hearts, our children. God will hear their prayers in English, too, I'm sure."

Life was good for the family in the weeks that followed. But in the city, the epidemic still raged, and nearly every week Papa brought news of some unfortunate neighbor that was stricken.

Especially they could not forget Lena. The girls wrote her weekly letters full of cheer and gossipy bits about their daily lives, with amusing little sketches drawn by Ella. But their letters were never answered. The children could not understand why. "She's probably still too weak to write," said Mama.

Several times Mama invited Uncle Hyman to come and visit. But he told Papa he couldn't. He said he wanted to be with Lena as much as possible.

Then one day he suddenly appeared, more shabby and unkempt than they had ever seen him. His stocky body seemed to have shrunk inside his rumpled suit. His round face was drawn, and his once merry eyes were sorrowful.

"How's Lena?" Mama asked.

"She's all right," he replied dully. "She'll be coming out of the hospital in a couple of days."

"Why, that's wonderful!" the children cried.

Uncle Hyman shook his head. "Lena won't marry me."

"What? What are you saying?" Mama was shocked.

Charlotte could feel her heart sink. "Doesn't she love you any more, Uncle Hyman?" she asked, her voice all trembly.

Uncle Hyman's hands rose and fell despairingly. "She does. But she won't marry me."

"But, why? Why?" Mama kept repeating. "I just don't understand!"

Uncle Hyman wiped his eyes with his sleeve. Then the words came haltingly. "We didn't tell anyone before — we weren't sure — we thought maybe —" He raised his head and talked only to Mama. "Lena's left leg is paralyzed. She'll have to wear a brace for the rest of her life!"

Mama rushed over and put her arm around her brother. "Oh, Hyman! To bear this alone — all this time."

For a while no one said anything. There didn't seem to be anything to say.

"So that's why she won't marry me," Uncle Hyman continued. "She feels she has no right to hold me."

"She's a proud girl, Hyman," declared Mama.

"Stubborn, you mean!" Uncle Hyman suddenly exploded.

"Perhaps," Mama answered, "but don't you see, Hyman, Lena's not the kind that wants pity."

"Who's pitying her? So she won't be able to run and jump

around! What do I care? I'm such a bargain myself? To me, Lena's the most wonderful happening in my whole life. All I know is I love her, and I want her to be my wife."

"Did you tell her that?" asked Ella.

"I tried. But she wouldn't listen. She said she never wants to see me again — just like that!"

Slowly Mama walked round and round the room, thinking. Everyone watched her. "Now listen carefully, Hyman," she said. "Just coming out of a hospital, Lena needs care. I'll have Papa bring her out this Friday. It will do her a world of good being here with me and the children. She can sit on the porch or out in the back garden."

"She wouldn't come."

"We'll make her," Mama said firmly. "When we're together I'll talk to her. Maybe I can make her understand how wrong she's acting."

Uncle Hyman flashed Mama a look of hope.

"But, Hyman," Mama added gently, "I think it'll be better if you don't come here — at least till I've had a chance to talk to her."

Uncle Hyman nodded his head and sighed heavily. "Yes, I understand. Only please, please, try!"

"I will, Hyman. I will," Mama assured him earnestly.

At Rockaway Beach

IN THE END it was Mama herself who finally brought Lena out. It was way past midnight when they arrived, and the children were all sound asleep in their beds.

In the morning, Sarah asked, "Did she come, Mama?"

"Yes. She's here."

They would have rushed from their beds, but Mama held up her hand warningly. She seemed to want to tell them something, but all she said was "Be careful, children."

It was a quiet group that followed Mama into the kitchen. Lena sat in the armchair by the open window, a light shawl thrown across her lap reaching to the floor. She had grown thin. Her face appeared almost gray, and deep shadows lay in the hollows beneath her eyes.

The sisters gathered around her with little Charlie grasping the arm of her chair. After a pause, Ella said, "We're so glad to see you, Lena."

Lena smiled at them. Her voice seemed strangely weak as she answered, "I'm happy to be with you all."

Immediately the girls were chattering about how much they were enjoying themselves, but Mama shooed them off. "Time for breakfast," she announced. "Besides, Lena needs rest and quiet."

Lena bent forward and took hold of Charlie's little fist. "And how's my little feller?" she asked. Charlie gazed up at her inquisitively. "Lena, Lena, Lena," he said sing-song as if the sound pleased him. He started to climb her lap. The shawl pulled away and slipped to the ground. The child's eye caught the gleam of shiny metal. "What you got on your leg?" he asked.

There was a dreadful moment of silence. The girls stared at the bulky frame of metal and leather straps.

Lena's lips pressed tightly together. A flicker of pain seemed to cross her face, but when she spoke, her voice was steady. "It's a brace, Charlie. My leg is sick. I can't walk without the brace." Quickly she picked up the shawl and covered her legs.

The girls sent appealing glances in Mama's direction. Mama came forward and took Charlie by the hand. "Raisins in your oatmeal this morning, Charlie. Just what you like."

The week that followed was a strain on everyone. Lena was learning to walk all over again, dragging the useless leg clumsily after her. It made the children sad. They could not help but remember the Lena who had been so keenly alive and gay. They soon realized that she hated to have anyone watch her limping along. So they would deliberately turn their backs and pretend to be busy elsewhere.

She never ventured beyond the front porch. Sometimes the girls would come upon her sitting there. A book or a bit of crocheting would lie neglected in her lap as she stared off into space. Sometimes, too, in the middle of the day, she'd go off to the bedroom to "lie down a little." But when she came out, her eyes would be red-rimmed and her nose all puffy.

Mama gave every spare moment to Lena, diverting her with chitchat and with work she could share in. Often when the children would return from the beach, they would find the two in earnest conversation. They could tell Mama was trying her best to set Lena right.

Time, the sunshine and fresh air, plus the loving care of the family, began slowly to work their miracles. One late afternoon the children found Mama and Lena sunning themselves in the backyard. "It's really nice here," Lena greeted them with a little laugh.

"It was very hard for her," Mama told them later. "Down all those porch steps! But she did it all by herself!"

Over the weekend, with Papa there, the house echoed with bright talk and merriment. He was in one of his comical moods, and he had them all in stitches. Once or twice even Lena couldn't help joining in the fun. "It's so good to hear her laugh again," Ella said.

A big event occurred in Ella's life the day Jules came up from the city. They spent the entire afternoon together on the beach. At supper time, while Jules was washing up, Lena asked jokingly, "You and your boy friend had a good time?"

"How could we?" Ella complained mildly. "With all my sisters butting in every minute!"

Later, in the cool of the evening, they went off for a walk by themselves. Ella felt pleasantly excited. Hand in hand, they strolled along the tree-lined streets. As they passed by the temple, the sound of beautiful singing floated out on the soft summer breeze.

"That's the High Holy Day Services they're practicing," Jules exclaimed. "I recognize it. I used to sing in a choir when I was a little boy."

"You did?" Ella was enchanted. "I didn't know you could sing."

"Uh-huh. I used to be a boy soprano." He grinned. "Until my voice changed."

"Let's go inside," Ella suggested. "I'm sure they won't mind."

They tiptoed in and sat down in the back row. Suddenly Ella gripped Jules's arm and whispered excitedly. "I know that music! We learned it in Hebrew School." Before they knew it, they were both singing right along with the choir.

Stirred by the beauty of the music and the joy of singing together, they completely forgot themselves. The choir leader caught the sound of singing coming from another part of the temple. Who would dare to interrupt his rehearsal? He motioned the choir to be still, and in the great big hall, only two voices went on.

Ella stopped right in the middle of a high note. She had suddenly realized that no one else was singing. "Come on, Jules!" she whispered in a panic. "Let's get out of here fast!" They edged their way out of the aisle.

"Stop!" the loud command halted them instantly. Embarrassed, Jules turned to apologize. But what was this he was hearing? "Come on down here to the piano! You have good voices, both of you. Come along!"

Ella caught Jules's hand and squeezed it hard. Together they ran forward.

"That was very nice. Very nice, indeed," the leader said smiling at them. "Can you sight read? You know — sing straight from a musical score?" he asked.

"I can," Ella said with a rush. "I've been taking singing lessons for quite a while." She pointed to Jules. "And he used to sing in a choir."

"Good. How'd you like to join our choir and sing with us during the High Holy Days?"

Ella's heart gave a skip and a jump. "Oh, I'd love it! How about you, Jules?"

"Sure. I'd like to get back to singing again."

"Well, then," Ella said, "when can we start?"

The director smiled at her eagerness. "How about right

now, and we'll see how you make out." He showed them to their places in the choir.

It was much later in the evening, and the younger children were already asleep. Mama, Henny, and Lena sat rocking on the front porch. "I wonder what can be keeping them?" Mama fretted. "They were just going for a walk."

"Young people like to take long walks," Lena answered.

"Here they come now," Henny called out.

Sure enough, there they were, racing headlong down the block. Up the porch steps they bounded. "The most marvelous thing — happened to us — tonight!" Ella panted. "You'll never guess!" And before anyone had a chance to reply, she proclaimed, "Meet the two newest members of the temple choir!"

"What's this?" Mama asked.

So Ella plunged into the story. When she had finished, Mama was bursting with pride. "Wait till Papa hears! Won't he be pleased!"

"You haven't heard it all, Mama," Ella went on. "We're going to be paid! Ten dollars each! Imagine that!"

"Wow!" gasped Henny.

"Of course we'll have to practice for the rest of the summer."

"We're going home right after Labor Day," Mama reminded her. "What's going to happen then?"

"I'll just ride back and forth for Sunday rehearsal. He said they'd pay the train fare."

"I see." Mama nodded. "It should be a wonderful experience. We'll talk about it some more. Now I think you'd better let Jules go home. He has a long trip."

"Well," Jules said as if he had just thought of it, "I'd better be going. Good-by. Thanks for everything."

"Come on, Jules. I'll see you to the corner," Ella said, linking her arm through his.

" 'Bye. And don't take another walk!" Henny called after them.

"That's a nice feller," Lena remarked as she watched them go. "So good-looking, too."

In a couple of minutes Ella came skipping back. She sat down on the porch steps. "It's been just the most perfect day!" she exclaimed blissfully. She stretched her arms high over her head. "I'm so happy!"

"Why shouldn't you be happy?" Lena said wistfully. Her head turned away. "You got something to look forward to."

"And so have you!" Mama said very loudly. "A good life together with a good man who loves you."

"I don't want to talk about it any more," Lena replied, pressing her lips together.

"You don't have to talk!" Mama shook her finger in Lena's face. "Just listen! How much longer will you allow your stubborn pride to make a fool of you? Hyman fell in love with you because you were good and kind and understanding. All this has not changed. Now at the first sign of a little trouble, you chase him away. Suppose it was Hyman who got sick? Is that what you would do — drop him like a hot potato?"

Never had Ella and Henny seen Mama so worked up before. She was awfully red in the face. They exchanged questioning glances. Should they go or stay? They sat still as mice, afraid to interrupt.

Lena was answering Mama. She sounded all choked up. "No — I never would have left him — but don't you understand? Like this — the way I am — Hyman is only sorry for me."

Mama slapped one hand against the other. "How can you be so selfish, Lena?"

Lena was taken aback. "Me! Selfish!"

"Yes! You're thinking only of how you feel. Why don't you stop for a minute and think about Hyman? Maybe he has feelings too. It nearly broke my heart to see how miserable he was the last time he was here." Mama put her hand on Lena's arm. She spoke almost pleadingly. "Don't you know Hyman would rather have you with a bad leg than anyone else in the whole world?"

Lena buried her face in her arms. Her wild sobbing cut into everyone's heart.

Mama let her cry for a while. Then she said softly, "Lena, you'll make Hyman a fine wife. I know you'll never be a burden. He's dying to see you, Lena. Don't you want to see him, too?"

Lena raised her tear-stained face. "Yes, I want to! I wanted to all the time!" She wavered. "You're sure it's the right thing to do?"

Mama kissed her wet cheek. "I'm sure."

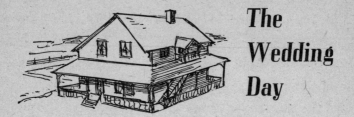

The Wedding Day

SUMMER was drawing to an end. Every day the newspapers said that the number of paralysis cases was growing less and less.

"I wish we didn't have to go back," Charlotte said. "It's so beautiful out here — the garden and the beach, and especially a house with a porch!"

"Yes," Ella agreed. "After this, the East Side's going to seem awfully crowded and noisy. Mama, why can't we move to the Bronx, like Lena?"

"Who can travel all the way down from the wilds of the Bronx?" remarked Papa. "As it is, I get up at five o'clock in the morning. There I'd have to get up in the middle of the night."

"Listen, Papa, maybe it's about time you stopped opening the shop so early," Mama told him. "It's not necessary. You

136

can open at seven or even eight and still manage to do the same amount of business."

Papa didn't answer, but the girls could tell he was giving it some thought. A little while later he said, "After all, we have so many relatives and friends and neighbors living on the East Side."

"The way they're all moving away, we won't have them much longer."

"And then there's my synagogue —"

"Plenty of other fine synagogues up in the Bronx," Mama argued back. "Look at the children. Just see how healthy and strong they have grown over the summer. If you want them to go on being that way, we must have a better place to live."

Papa was listening intently. Could it be that he was agreeing with Mama, the children wondered? Mama kept on talking. "The children are growing up. We'll be needing a larger apartment."

"Well," Papa put her off, "we'll think about it. Anyway, there's plenty of time. The holidays are coming soon, and I want to pray in my own synagogue, at least this year. Then there's the election. If we move away before, I lose my vote. And every citizen should vote. Afterwards, we'll see."

So Mama and the girls had to be content with that.

Charlotte threw open the closet door. "You lovely, lovely wedding dresses!" she exclaimed rapturously. "We're going to wear you after all! Did you miss us while we were in Rockaway?" Breathlessly, she added, "I wonder, can you wait till tomorrow?"

Henny laughed. "Do you expect the dresses to talk back?" And the laughter ran around the room.

"Charlotte," Mama called out, "get away from the closet and come over here right away. You're next."

Mama poured some kerosene over Charlotte's head and began to rub it briskly with her finger tips. "Ooh, Ma! It makes my scalp tingle," Charlotte fretted.

"I know, but kerosene keeps the scalp clean and healthy. Tomorrow morning when we wash it out, your hair will shine like satin."

One after the other, the girls received the same treatment. Then, their heads tightly swathed in a towel, and smelling to high heaven, they sat around chattering about the exciting event on the morrow.

"I'd better get out my Prince Albert," Papa said. The suit lay packed away in moth balls and was taken out only for very special occasions.

Mama said, "You looked so handsome in it the day we got

married. Do you think it'll still fit?" Everyone knew she was just teasing. Hard work kept Papa's figure slim as a young man's.

As Papa hung the suit out on the line to get rid of the odor of moth balls, Henny put her fingers to her nose. "What with our heads and Papa's suit, going to a wedding is a smelly business," she remarked.

At last it was the afternoon of the wedding. Papa stood preening himself before the full length mirror. The girls smiled to one another. He held himself very straight. They watched him carefully fix the white flower in his buttonhole. He turned slowly, looking at himself from all sides. Nodding to the mirror in pleased satisfaction, he swung his high silk hat onto his head.

"Well, I'm ready," he announced. "Pretty handsome feller, don't you think?"

"You really look very distinguished," Ella told him, and the girls all agreed.

Then Mama swept into the room for her turn at the mirror.

"Look at Mama! She looks so young and pretty!" exclaimed Sarah.

The children danced around Mama admiring her shiny

blue satin dress, all tucked in the blouse and soft flowing in the skirt. A corsage of tiny pink roses that Uncle Hyman had sent made a charming finishing touch.

As for the girls, they were like a bouquet of flowers themselves in their white lace-trimmed dresses with pastel colored sashes and hair ribbons to match.

Papa beamed with approval. "We're certainly a stylish-looking family."

"Except Charlie," Mama said. "He's not dressed up yet. So he shouldn't have time to get dirty," she explained.

Charlie hated getting all dressed up. But despite his twisting and turning, Mama had him ready at last. He looked so adorable in his velvet suit with his blond hair slicked down like a big boy's that the girls all wanted to hug him. But Mama said, "No. No mussing him up!"

Papa peered out of the window. "Here comes the carriage!" he shouted. "Come on. Let's go!"

Swish, swish, the petticoats rustled as the family paraded down the stairs. "I still can't see why we need a carriage just to go across the street," Mama declared. "Such a foolish waste of money!"

"Hyman wanted to please the children."

"Oh, Mama, it's stylish to come in a carriage," Ella said.

"Of course," added Charlotte. "When you step down from a carriage, you're like a king or queen, with everybody standing around and staring."

"Papa, please tell the driver to go around the block first," begged Henny.

"Yes, Papa, please!" the others chimed in.

The driver, an old man in a shabby suit and dusty cap, didn't even bother to turn around when Papa tapped him on the shoulder. He seemed bored with the whole business. "Okay," he replied to Papa. "Let's go."

"Such a poor old horse," Sarah said. "He's so skinny, his bones are sticking out. Can he pull all of us?"

Charlotte wrinkled up her nose. "It smells musty in here."

"Giddyap!" the driver called out. The carriage springs creaked and squeaked as the horse plodded slowly around the block and stopped in front of the hall.

Papa jumped out and helped his family down. All the girls put on a grand and haughty air. This time they were the lucky ones to disappear inside the big hall while others stood curiously outside. They turned their heads this way and that, smiling graciously. Then, like royal princesses, they promenaded up the steps and through the door.

They entered an enormous room which, to the children, seemed as big and beautiful as a palace.

Everywhere artificial flowers bloomed in tall vases. From the high ceiling hung crystal chandeliers scattering their sparkling lights over the glassy smooth floor. Gilt painted chairs with worn red plush seats were lined up like soldiers against the walls. The tall windows were draped in faded red velvet hangings. Between them, long mirrors reflected the girls' likenesses over and over down the full length of the hall. Gertie stopped before one which had a large irregular crack running down its center. "Ooh, look!" she exclaimed, "I have two pieces of face!"

The relatives were greeting one another, faces wreathed in smiles. Men shook hands heartily. Women embraced and planted kisses on the children's cheeks.

Uncle Hyman was busy bobbing in and out of the small groups of guests, the long coat tails of his rented dress suit flapping behind. "If those coat tails were just a tiny bit longer, they could use Uncle Hyman instead of a broom," Henny said, giggling. Just then Uncle Hyman caught sight of the family and came a-running.

Papa slapped him affectionately on the back. "Well, Hyman," he said. "This is your big day!"

"Yes! Yes!" Uncle Hyman beamed. His face was redder than ever. Beads of perspiration were gathered in small blobs beneath the brim of his top hat. As he talked, the stiff bosom of his white shirt kept popping up. "It won't stay down," he complained. "It's a good thing I don't have to be dressed like this every day."

"So don't breathe so hard," Papa said, laughing.

"Where's Lena?" Gertie piped up. "I want to see the bride."

"I'd like to see her myself, Gertie," answered Uncle Hyman.

"She's in that little room over there with some of the women. I have to wait till the ceremony, but you can go in right now."

In the little room, Lena sat enthroned on a high-backed arm chair. Her white satin gown fell in graceful folds, forming a wide circle on the carpeted floor. A delicate wreath of blossoms entwined in her hair made a lovely frame for her face, and from it a filmy white veil floated. In her gloved hands, she held a bouquet of white roses tied with satin ribbon streamers.

"How could we ever have thought her plain?" Ella caught herself thinking. She studied the bride's face. It seemed aglow with light as if happiness had woven a magic spell. "Lena, you're beautiful!" she cried.

Lena held out her arms to the children. They went over to her cautiously, fearful of crushing the flowers and her gown. She kissed each of them, smiling into their adoring faces. She held Mama's hand in hers for a long time, and her eyes became all misty. Finally she said, "Go, children. Enjoy yourselves."

"Lena looks pale," Charlotte observed as they left the room.

"That's because she hasn't eaten a thing the whole day," Henny explained.

"She hasn't!" Gertie asked, astonished.

"Uh huh. It's the custom. The bride and groom must always fast on their wedding day."

"That's right," said Ella. "The fasting is supposed to cleanse the soul. Then to cleanse her body, the bride also goes to the *mikvah* (pool) before her wedding."

"Why can't she stay home and take a bath in her own house?" inquired Charlotte.

"Well, it's not just an ordinary bath," Ella went on to explain. "The women go to a bath house. They go down the steps of the pool and duck themselves under the water. Then prayers are recited over them — by some older woman, usually."

Back in the hall the girls heard the sound of sprightly music. "Where is it coming from?" Sarah asked. "I don't see anybody."

Ella pointed to a small balcony in the rear. "There they are. Up there."

Just then Henny spied Jules threading his way towards them through the crowd. Her eyebrows arched inquiringly. "What's he doing here?"

"Lena invited him," Ella replied.

Jules looked at her. "You're very pretty tonight, Ella," he said shyly. Quickly he added, "I mean — you all look nice."

"We all thank you," Ella answered gaily. As the music started up again, Jules asked her to dance, and off they went.

"Come on, Sarah. Let's you and me dance," Henny cried, grabbing her around the waist and whirling her away.

Charlotte and Gertie weren't dancing. They stood by at the end of the hall, enviously watching several of their boy cousins. The boys were playing a most delightful game. Taking a running start, whiz-z-z! each slid down the length of the room, bumping into the dancers right and left. Charlotte sniffed loudly. "Look at them! They don't even know how to behave at a wedding!"

But the boys' fun didn't last long. A smart slap on the backside from a watchful Uncle Solomon, and the wonderful game came to a sudden end.

The musicians struck up a waltz. "Gracious lady," Papa bowed very low, "may I have the honor?"

Mama curtsied and replied "Why, thank you, kind sir."

Papa held out his arms. "We'll show the children what real dancing looks like," he declared.

As Papa swung Mama round and round to the tune of the old-fashioned waltz, they seemed so young and carefree that the children were bursting with love and pride. "Aren't they handsome!" Sarah cried, and even Charlie clapped his hands.

Soon his tiny feet went pattering after them. In and out amongst the dancers he wove, till at last he reached his dear ones. Chuckling, he clung to Mama's skirts, shaking himself up and down to imitate her dancing steps. Papa picked him up, and the dancing circle of three continued waltzing around the floor.

The hall grew warm. The hot and thirsty guests crowded around the refreshment table. Cases of celery tonic and seltzer, mounds of sponge cake and honey cake, wine and schnapps — they made short work of all.

Someone struck several loud chords on the piano. "The ceremony! The ceremony is beginning!" the loud whisper ran around the room. Hurriedly the guests found seats. At a signal, the ushers brought in the *huppah* signifying the house in which the couple would dwell. It was shaped like a canopy in vivid red satin, exquisitely embroidered with gold thread, and supported by wooden poles, one at each corner. It was held aloft by four wedding guests.

The lights were dimmed. A hush fell over the assembly. In the doorway the wedding procession stood ready. The wedding march began.

There was no mother to lead her son to the altar; so Mama walked beside Uncle Hyman down the hall and under the *huppah*. There was no father, either, to give away the bride; so Papa acted the part. The veil let down over her face and her gown trailing gracefully behind, Lena leaned on Papa's arm.

Slowly, haltingly, she began the long walk. The guests looked on sympathetically as, somewhat clumsily, she dragged her lame leg. But Lena was unaware of anyone. Her head was high and proud. She looked only toward the *huppah,* where Uncle Hyman waited. Bravely she tried to adjust to the rhythm of the music.

"Psst, psst! Musicians!" Someone signaled frantically. "Slower, slower!"

The musicians understood. The measures of the wedding march lengthened. Behind Lena the bridesmaids and their partners slowly followed.

At last Lena was under the *huppah.* The music stopped. Seven times around the groom the bride was led, and the marriage service began.

The rabbi lifted up a goblet of wine, reciting the blessing. He offered the goblet to the bride and groom, and each took a sip. A ring of plain, unadorned gold was placed on Lena's left hand. The marriage contract was given to her, and the rabbi recited seven nuptial blessings. He raised a second goblet of wine, intoning a blessing. Once again the couple drank. These two goblets represent the cups of joy and sorrow.

A glass was set down on the floor. Uncle Hyman had to crush it with his heel for good luck. He raised his foot. The sisters held their breath. If he could smash the glass with one blow, that would mean extra special good luck! Down came the heel, and the glass shattered into pieces. From all around loud exclamations of rejoicing were heard.

The rabbi gave the couple his blessing, and Uncle Hyman kissed the bride. Suddenly a skylight window was thrown open, and from a wire cage, pigeons were released. They came whirling down in a rush of wings, circling round and round the *huppah*.

Once more the chandeliers were ablaze with light. The musicians burst into a lively melody, and the hall resounded with congratulations and well-wishing. *"Mazel tov! Mazel tov!* (Good luck! Good luck!)" The people rushed forward to shake the hand of the groom and to kiss the bride — husband and wife, now!

Dance! Dance! the music seemed to call urgently. "It's a *kazatske* (Russian folk dance)!"

The old folks sprang from their seats, and soon small circles of dancers pranced about. They circled to the right, then to the left, tripping in to the center and out. Looping arms with their partners, they spun around, first one way and then the other. Women held their skirts wide. Men slapped their hands and stamped their feet. Faster and livelier went the music. Faster and livelier went the dancers. Such interesting steps, half remembered from dances done in the villages in the old country, half invented on the spur of the moment. The circles widened. They became one big circle as little children and grown-ups joined in. Finally the music stopped, and the exhausted dancers, breathing hard, stood around wiping their flushed faces with their handkerchiefs.

An elderly man wearing overalls and a painter's cap entered, carrying a covered basket and a long pole to which a net was attached. He came to a halt in the very center of the hall, beneath the skylight. The children rushed over to watch as he deftly reached up with his pole and snared the pigeons. One by one he popped the birds into the basket.

But there was one rebel who refused to be caught. He kept darting from one side of the skylight to the other. The children were delighted with his antics. They skipped about, laughing boisterously, and offered all kinds of advice to the bird-catcher.

"He wants to stay for supper," Charlotte cried. "Why don't they let him?"

The old man tired. Muttering to himself, he went out with the pole and returned, dragging a tall ladder after him. He set the ladder up right in the midst of all the assembled company and climbed to the topmost rung. Seizing hold of the lone pigeon, he thrust it into his basket. Then off he went, ladder, basket, pigeons, and all.

There was a loud fanfare from the musicians. Grownups and children arranged themselves into two zigzaggy lines. Round the hall they paraded, out into the foyer and down the stairs to the dining room. Uncle Hyman and Lena, already at their places, graciously greeted the guests. On a little table in front of them, the wedding cake stood, a white tower of beauty. The girls inspected it from all sides before sitting down.

"Isn't it gorgeous!" Charlotte marveled. "It's a shame to cut it up."

The wedding supper! Fricassee, soup with noodles and *mandel* (croutons), roast chicken, stuffed *derma, kashe* (buckwheat groats), carrots and peas, hot tea, and, last, pieces of the luscious wedding cake.

Henny was in seventh heaven. As each course made its appearance, she announced blissfully, "This I like!" It took a long, long time to eat, for in between there was much singing and speechmaking.

Wearied by the lateness of the hour and all the noise and excitement, Charlie fell fast asleep. "I'll take him upstairs, Mama," Ella offered, and carried her little brother up two flights to the babies' room. An old lady wearing a big white apron sat guard over other little ones who had already succumbed to sleepiness. In their crumpled finery, all shapes and sizes, the babies lay crosswise on two large beds.

Late into the night the festivities went on. The people danced till the soles of their feet burned. Till their mouths ached with the constant jabbering. Till their bodies sagged with fatigue. When the celebration finally came to an end, Mama's girls were very glad that they lived just across the street.

Home at last, eyes half shut, they stumbled into bed. "Wasn't it just the most beautiful — beautiful —" Ella's yawn was wide. "There's just nothing like a — big — wedding —" Her last words could scarcely be heard. But it did not matter. Everyone was asleep.

The End
and the
Beginning

ALONE IN THE ISLAND of her bed, Sarah was glad for once that Ella went to bed later than she. How she had longed for this moment! All day, amid the commotion and rush, the constant coming and going of neighbors and relatives, she had carried around the awful hollowness inside her. If only she could cry it away, she thought. But in front of everybody! How could she? Wait till you're in bed, she kept telling herself. Well, it was safe to let go, now. She buried her head in the pillow and waited for the tears to come.

Sadness lay in the bed with her, and yet, oddly enough, the tears refused to flow. She found herself thinking about her sisters. They were unusually quiet. Were they upset, too? Slowly she raised her head.

In the kitchen, Mama, Papa, and Ella were busy with last-minute wrapping and packing. It was comforting to hear their voices.

Sarah sat up and leaned against the bedpost. She let her eyes wander over the dear familiar place. The dressers looked queer without the delicate lacy scarves, without all the little knick-knacks and brushes and combs. The walls, now bare of mirrors and pictures; the window, curtainless, made the room seem barren. In the corner stood barrels filled to the brim with dishes and glassware.

Charlotte's voice broke the stillness. "It'll seem funny living someplace else."

"Yes," agreed Gertie. "We've lived here our whole lives!"

"Well, it's about time we made a change," Henny said cheerfully. "Mama and Papa kept talking about it, but I honestly never thought we'd do it. I'm sure glad. I'm sort of tired of this old place. Doing the same old things and seeing the same old faces all the time."

Oh, thought Sarah, how could anybody ever grow tired of the things that were part of her? Knowing things and people so well made them dear to you. Taking on new ways and new friends, that was hard — almost terrifying. "Henny," she asked wonderingly, "won't you even miss your friends?"

"My gracious! We're not moving to Europe! It's just a subway ride to the Bronx. We'll be coming down to see them. Besides," Henny added, "you can always make new friends."

"Ye—es," Gertie's voice sounded troubled, "but we're so used to it here. Now we'll have to go to a new school and — "

"Bah!" interrupted Henny. "Schools are all alike. All they are is teachers and studying and homework — and tests!"

The bedroom door opened wide. "Still awake, children?" Mama called in. She entered the room and sat down on Sarah's bed. "Too excited to sleep? Me and Papa, too!" She hugged her arms and gave a little shiver. "It's cold in here. That's one thing we won't have to worry about in our new home — steam heat in every room." She sighed happily. "Imagine! No more ashes to clean out."

"No more nasty stove polishings, either!" Henny exclaimed with glee.

Mama laughed. "Tell you what," she suggested. "Let's all go into the warm kitchen. We can sit around and talk for a while. I'll make some hot cocoa. Then maybe we'll feel more like going to sleep.

No one needed a second invitation. Soon they were all seated around the big table sipping the rich, sweet cocoa.

"You're going to love it in the Bronx, children," Mama began. "Everything's so new and clean. And you won't even have to go to a playground. Our house has a back garden."

"Like in Rockaway, Mama?" Charlotte asked.

"Yes — only even bigger."

"Tell again about the house," begged Gertie.

So Mama told. "Well, it's also a private house — just two floors. The landlord lives downstairs, and we're one flight up. There's carpet in the halls and on the stairs."

"Carpet!" "Mama, how grand!"

"And don't forget," Papa said impressively, "seven rooms, with electric light!"

Charlotte couldn't get over it. "Nobody on the East Side ever lived in seven rooms!"

"With electric light! A regular palace!" cried Gertie.

Mama was elated. Sarah could tell by the merry lilt in her voice. She felt her own spirits lifting a little. "Seven rooms! Mama," she said, "we don't have nearly enough furniture."

"Oh, but we have!" Papa replied, the crinkly lines around his eyes deepening. "Mama and I were saving this for a surprise. We bought a dining room set, a desk with a chair to match, and a brand new couch for the front room, and I can't remember what other things."

There was a shower of ohs and ahs and dozens of questions from the girls. Finally Charlotte inquired, "Papa, are we rich now?"

Papa paused. His face and voice grew sober. "If you mean,

my child, do we have more money, the answer is yes. When Mama and I first came to America, things were very hard for us. But this is truly a wonderful country. Here everyone has a chance to better himself. And God has helped also. He blessed our home with six wonderful children, and all the time he provided — more than provided — for all of us. So for a long, long time, we have saved for this day.

"But one thing you must always remember. We have never been poor. We have always been very, very rich. And do you know why? Because we have always had each other."

Mama's face also grew serious. She began to talk as if she were thinking out loud. "On the East Side, we were mostly with people of our own faith. I mean Jews like ourselves who came over from Europe. We spoke a common language — Jewish. We all went to the synagogue together. We celebrated the same holidays. Now we're going to live together with all kinds of people, Jewish and gentile. Our new landlord is a gentile.

"Yes," Papa said, "in some ways, to you and me, Mama, it'll seem more like a strange land than when we first came to America."

"Papa, it's good this way," declared Mama. "It's good that people should learn to know and understand one another." Her eyes twinkled as she added, "and you don't have to worry. There are Jewish stores in the neighborhood. We'll still be able to buy *bagel* and *lox* for Sunday morning breakfast."

Thus the family sat around and talked long after the last drop of cocoa was gone. Mama stood up and said, "Now, I think we'd better go to sleep. We have a lot to do tomorrow!"

On the way to bed, Gertie said to Charlotte, "I just can't wait to see the new place, can you?"

"Let's fall asleep right away," Charlotte answered. "That'll make the morning come faster."

Morning came quickly enough. It seemed no time at all before Mama was shaking them. "Up, children! The moving men will be here any minute!" The girls jumped out of their beds and hurried with their dressing and gulped their breakfast. They were tying up the last bundles just as the moving men arrived.

Up and down the men went, their bodies bent almost double under the weight of the family belongings. Charlie kept getting in everyone's way, frisking about like a small puppy.

For the last time the family walked through the empty flat, their footsteps re-echoing hollowly. Each heart was full of memories of the happy years spent within these walls. "It was a good home," Mama said. "But you'll see, our new home will be even better."

When they came downstairs, the moving men were already
finished loading. They were tying the rear of the wagon criss-
cross with heavy ropes. Friends and neighbors were gathered
around the stoop to wish them Godspeed. "Good-by! Good-by!"
"We'll miss you!" There were many farewell kisses and tears.
"Come and see us once in a while! Don't forget!"

The driver flicked the reins against the horses' flanks.
"Giddyap!" With a jar, the van moved away from the curb and
rumbled down the street. Silently everyone watched it depart.

There was one last, lingering look for everyone at the small
house on the narrow street that once had been home. "Good-by,
dear old house, good-by." Charlotte made a little song of it.

Gertie chimed in. "Good-by, Mr. Basch's grocery store! "Good-by, wedding hall!"

"Come," Mama said, taking hold of Charlie's hand. "We'd better go. We want to be there when the moving men arrive."

They reached the corner. Sarah turned back once more. "We won't forget you. Good-by, good-by, dear East Side!"

They rounded the corner. A fresh wind set Henny's curls dancing. "Hello, Bronx! Here we come!" she yelled.

And the sisters echoed, "Here we come!"